Texas Christmas Tales

The Great Texas Line Press
Fort Worth, Texas

© Copyright: Great Texas Line Press

Bulk sales of books from the Great Texas Line are available at special discounts for fund-raising, promotions and premiums.

Great Texas Line Press
Post Office Box 11105
Fort Worth, Texas 76110
greattexas@hotmail.com
www.greattexasline.com
Tel. (800) 73TEXAS

ISBN No. 978-1-8925882-1-0
Library of Congress Central Number: 2011933147

Cover Design: Jared Stone
Illustrations, Cover & Inside: Mark Hoffer
Page Design: Debbie Ford
Printer: Hanson Printing, Fort Worth

Printed in Texas by Texans

Table of Contents

Introduction

As a lifelong reader I've constantly marveled at the literary world's never-ending flow of Christmas stories and found myself often wondering about their origins. As a writer I know something of dreaded deadlines and thus am aware that, for any book or story with a holiday setting to make it to publication day on time, it had to have been written long before frost stilled the night air, snow warnings were issued, gaily-colored lights went onto rooftops and shopping centers from sea to shining sea were advertising simultaneous visits from Santa.

My guess is that everyone from Charles Dickens to Chris Van Allsburg at some point simply sat and wiped the hot summer sweat from their brows and thought to themselves, "Okay, its time to get into the Christmas spirit and create ol' Ebenezer Scrooge and Bob Cratchit, or a magical train that travels through the night to the North Pole."

I know for a fact that Fort Worth's Jeff Guinn wrote much of his best-seller *The Autobiography of Santa Claus* while dressed in running shorts and T-shirts with the air conditioner straining mightily to ward off 100-degree August days.

That, I believe, is how great writers' imaginations work, not so much by season but rather with a strong and ever-present sense of what makes a good story, regardless of the date on their office calendar. If it happens to be set at a time when everyone's humming "Jingle Bells," so much the better.

And bless their hearts and inventive minds for being foresighted enough to provide us enduring stories for the Yuletide season.

And while you're at it, give a grateful nod to the men whose stories you are about to read on the following pages. Regardless of what season it was when the idea to write "The Golden Shadows Old West Museum" and "The Night the Wise Men Sucker-Punched the Elf" struck Mike Blackman, they read as if they were crafted on some bygone Christmas Eve with visions of great humor and irony dancing merrily in his head. Did O. Henry write his Texas cowboy story called "A Chaparral Christmas Gift" in December? Who cares? Though far different from his classic "The Gift of the Magi," it is still pure and memorable O. Henry. And it seems clear that John Henry Faulk's moving "A Christmas Story" was written after the ornaments were taken down, but it has an endearing quality that has made it an evergreen.

If, in the spirit of the season, you'll allow me a prediction, it is my belief that none of these stories are one-time reads. They will return to your thoughts as each new Christmas season arrives. You'll read them again and again, to yourself and to others. That's what this time of giving is all about. And these writers have come bearing wonderful gifts.

— *Carlton Stowers*

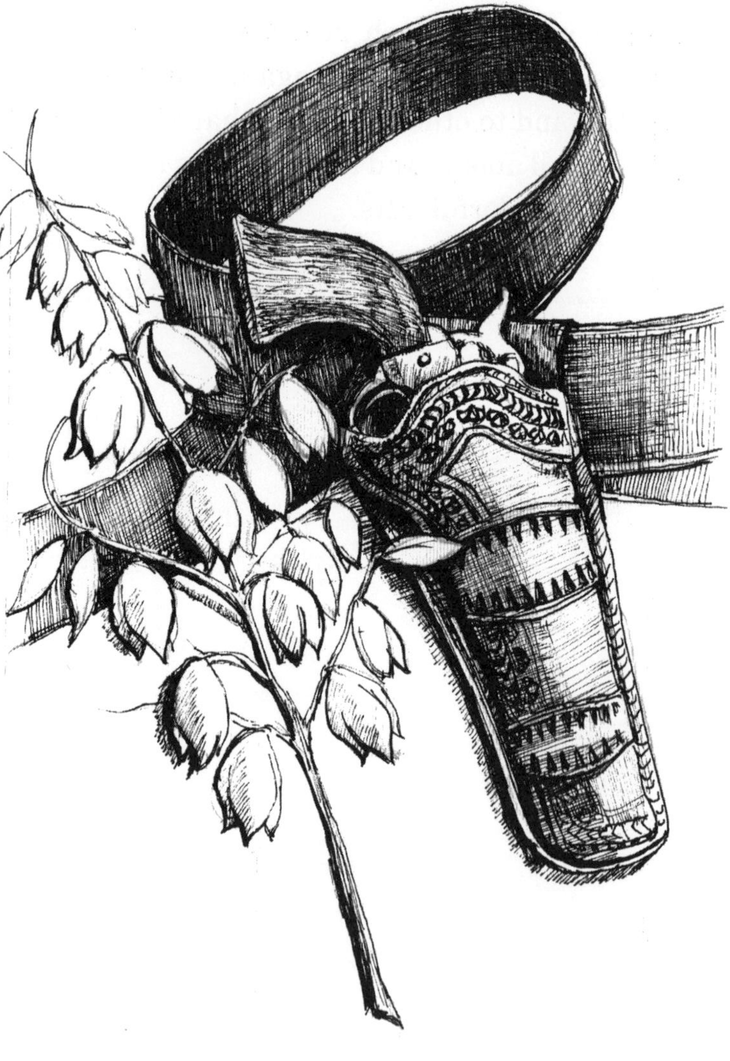

A Chaparral Christmas Gift

By O. Henry

The Gift of the Magi *wasn't O. Henry's only Christmas story. He penned one set in Texas ranch country that was included in his* Whirligigs *collection published in 1910, the year of his death. Texas was where William Sidney Porter, better known under his pen name, O. Henry, began his writing career, and he knew whereof he wrote in this story, as he lived and worked on a sheep ranch in La Salle County southwest of San Antonio when he first came to Texas from his home state of North Carolina, in 1882.*

———————

The original cause of the trouble was about 20 years in growing.

At the end of that time it was worth it.

Had you lived anywhere within fifty miles of Sundown Ranch you would have heard of it. It possessed a quantity of jet-black hair, a pair of extremely frank, deep-brown eyes and a laugh that rippled across the prairie like the sound of a hidden brook. The name of it was Rosita McMullen; and she was the daughter of old man McMullen of the Sundown Sheep Ranch.

There came riding on red roan steeds—or, to be more explicit, on a paint and a flea-bitten sorrel—two wooers. One was Madison Lane, and the other was the Frio Kid. But at that time they did not call him the Frio Kid, for he had not earned the honors of special nomenclature. His name was simply Johnny McRoy.

It must not be supposed that these two were the sum of the agreeable Rosita's admirers. The bronchos of a dozen others champed their bits at the long hitching rack of the Sundown Ranch. Many were the sheeps'-eyes that were cast in those savannas that did not belong to the flocks of Dan McMullen. But of all the cavaliers, Madison Lane and Johnny McRoy galloped far ahead, wherefore they are to be chronicled.

Madison Lane, a young cattleman from the Nueces country, won the race. He and Rosita were married one Christmas day. Armed, hilarious, vociferous, magnanimous, the cowmen and the sheepmen, laying aside their hereditary hatred, joined forces to celebrate the occasion. Sundown Ranch was sonorous with the cracking of jokes and sixshooters, the shine of buckles and bright eyes, the outspoken congratulations of the herders of kine.

But while the wedding feast was at its liveliest there descended upon it Johnny McRoy, bitten by jealousy, like one possessed.

"I'll give you a Christmas present," he yelled, shrilly, at the door, with his .45 in his hand. Even then he had some reputation as an offhand shot.

His first bullet cut a neat underbit in Madison Lane's right ear. The barrel of his gun moved an inch. The next shot would have been the bride's had not Carson, a sheepman, possessed a mind with triggers somewhat well oiled and in repair. The guns of the wedding party had been hung, in their belts, upon nails in the wall when they sat at table, as a concession to good taste. But Carson, with great promptness, hurled his plate of roast venison and frijoles at McRoy, spoiling his aim. The second bullet, then, only shattered the white petals of a Spanish dagger flower suspended two feet above Rosita's head.

The guests spurned their chairs and jumped for their weapons. It was considered an improper act to shoot the bride and groom at a wedding. In about six seconds there were twenty or so bullets due to be whizzing in the direction of Mr. McRoy.

"I'll shoot better next time," yelled Johnny; "and there'll be a next time." He backed rapidly out the door.

Carson, the sheepman, spurred on to attempt further exploits by the success of his plate-throwing, was first to reach the door. McRoy's bullet from the darkness laid him low.

The cattlemen then swept out upon him, calling for vengeance, for, while the slaughter of a sheepman has not always lacked condonement, it was a decided misdemeanour in this instance. Carson was innocent; he was no accomplice at

11

the matrimonial proceedings; nor had anyone heard him quote the line "Christmas comes but once a year" to the guests.

But the sortie failed in its vengeance. McRoy was on his horse and away, shouting back curses and threats as he galloped into the concealing chaparral.

That night was the birthnight of the Frio Kid. He became the "bad man" of that portion of the State. The rejection of his suit by Miss McMullen turned him to a dangerous man. When officers went after him for the shooting of Carson, he killed two of them, and entered upon the life of an outlaw. He became a marvellous shot with either hand. He would turn up in towns and settlements, raise a quarrel at the slightest opportunity, pick off his man and laugh at the officers of the law. He was so cool, so deadly, so rapid, so inhumanly blood-thirsty that none but faint attempts were ever made to capture him. When he was at last shot and killed by a little one-armed Mexican who was nearly dead himself from fright, the Frio Kid had the deaths of eighteen men on his head. About half of these were killed in fair duels depending upon the quickness of the draw. The other half were men whom he assassinated from absolute wantonness and cruelty.

Many tales are told along the border of his impudent courage and daring. But he was not one of the breed of desperadoes who have seasons of generosity and even of softness. They say he never had mercy on the object of his anger. Yet at this and every Christmastide it is well to give each one credit, if it can be done, for whatever speck of good he may have possessed. If the Frio Kid ever did a kindly act or felt a throb of generosity in his heart it was once at such a time and season, and this is the way it happened.

One who has been crossed in love should never breathe the odour from the blossoms of the ratama tree. It stirs the memory to a dangerous degree.

One December in the Frio country there was a ratama tree in full bloom, for the winter had been as warm as springtime. That way rode the Frio Kid and his satellite and co-murderer, Mexican Frank. The kid reined in his mustang, and sat in his saddle, thoughtful and grim, with dangerously narrowing eyes. The rich, sweet scent touched him somewhere beneath his ice and iron.

"I don't know what I've been thinking about, Mex," he remarked in his usual mild drawl, "to have forgot all about a Christmas present I got to give. I'm going to ride over to-morrow night and shoot Madison Lane in his own house. He got my girl—Rosita would have had me if he hadn't cut into the game. I wonder why I happened to overlook it up to now?"

13

"Ah, shucks, Kid," said Mexican, "don't talk foolishness. You know you can't get within a mile of Mad Lane's house to-morrow night. I see old man Allen day before yesterday, and he says Mad is going to have Christmas doings at his house. You remember how you shot up the festivities when Mad was married, and about the threats you made? Don't you suppose Mad Lane'll kind of keep his eye open for a certain Mr. Kid? You plumb make me tired, Kid, with such remarks."

"I'm going," repeated the Frio Kid, without heat, "to go to Madison Lane's Christmas doings, and kill him. I ought to have done it a long time ago. Why, Mex, just two weeks ago I dreamed me and Rosita was married instead of her and him; and we was living in a house, and I could see her smiling at me, and—oh! h---l, Mex, he got her; and I'll get him—yes, sir, on Christmas Eve he got her, and then's when I'll get him."

"There's other ways of committing suicide," advised Mexican. "Why don't you go and surrender to the sheriff?"

"I'll get him," said the Kid.

Christmas Eve fell as balmy as April. Perhaps there was a hint of far-away frostiness in the air, but it tingles like seltzer, perfumed faintly with late prairie blossoms and the mesquite grass.

When night came the five or six rooms of the ranch-house were brightly lit. In one room was a Christmas tree, for the Lanes had a boy of three, and a dozen or more guests were expected from the nearer ranches.

At nightfall Madison Lane called aside Jim Belcher and three other cowboys employed on his ranch.

"Now, boys," said Lane, "keep your eyes open. Walk around the house and watch the road well. All of you know the 'Frio Kid,' as they call him now, and if you see him, open fire on him without asking any questions. I'm not afraid of his coming around, but Rosita is. She's been afraid he'd come in on us every Christmas since we were married."

The guests had arrived in buckboards and on horseback, and were making themselves comfortable inside.

The evening went along pleasantly. The guests enjoyed and praised Rosita's excellent supper, and afterward the men scattered in groups about the rooms or on the broad "gallery," smoking and chatting.

The Christmas tree, of course, delighted the youngsters, and above all were they pleased when Santa Claus himself in magnificent white beard and furs appeared and began to distribute the toys.

"It's my papa," announced Billy Sampson, aged six. "I've seen him wear 'em before."

Berkly, a sheepman, an old friend of Lane, stopped Rosita as she was passing by him on the gallery, where he was sitting smoking.

"Well, Mrs. Lane," said he, "I suppose by this Christmas you've gotten over being afraid of that fellow McRoy, haven't you? Madison and I have talked about it, you know."

"Very nearly," said Rosita, smiling, "but I am still nervous sometimes. I shall never forget that awful time when he came so near to killing us."

"He's the most cold-hearted villain in the world," said Berkly. "The citizens all along the border ought to turn out and hunt him down like a wolf."

"He has committed awful crimes," said Rosita, "but—I—don't—know. I think there is a spot of good somewhere in everybody. He was not always bad—that I know."

Rosita turned into the hallway between the rooms. Santa Claus, in muffling whiskers and furs, was just coming through.

"I heard what you said through the window, Mrs. Lane," he said. "I was just going down in my pocket for a Christmas present for your husband. But I've left one for you, instead. It's in the room to your right."

"Oh, thank you, kind Santa Claus," said Rosita, brightly.

Rosita went into the room, while Santa Claus stepped into the cooler air of the yard.

She found no one in the room but Madison.

"Where is my present that Santa said he left for me in here?" she asked.

"Haven't seen anything in the way of a present," said her husband, laughing, "unless he could have meant me."

The next day Gabriel Radd, the foreman of the X O Ranch, dropped into the post-office at Loma Alta.

"Well, the Frio Kid's got his dose of lead at last," he remarked to the postmaster.

"That so? How'd it happen?"

"One of old Sanchez's Mexican sheep herders did it!—think of it! the Frio Kid killed by a sheep herder! The Mexican saw him riding along past his camp about twelve o'clock last night, and was so skeered that he up with a Winchester and let him have it. Funniest part of it was that the Kid was dressed all up with white Angora-skin whiskers and a regular Santy Claus rig-out from head to foot. Think of the Frio Kid playing Santy!"

17

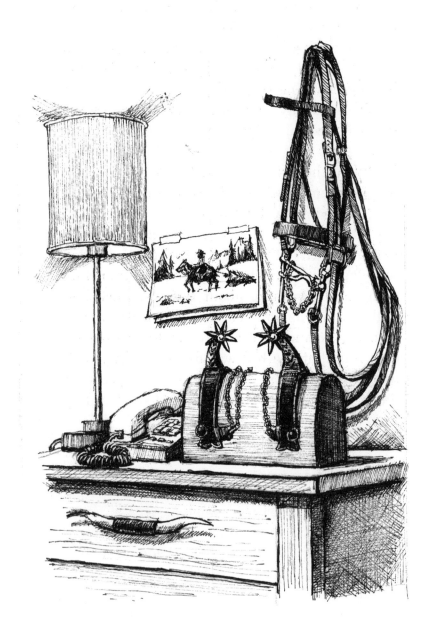

The Golden Shadows Old West Museum

By Mike Blackman

This story was named best short story of 1973 by the Texas Institute of Letters. It first appeared in The Ohio Journal, *the literary review of Ohio State University, where the West-Texas-born Blackman attended graduate school. In 1989, Texas author-playwright Larry L. King turned it into a play that has since been performed in numerous cities. In 1994, TCU Press published both the story and the play as part of its Texas Series collection. A former executive editor for the Fort Worth Star-Telegram, Blackman is the Fred Hartman Professor of Journalism at his alma mater, Baylor University, and one of the state's most revered and respected journalists.*

————————

The lobby of Golden Shadows Rest & Care Home brought little excitement or comfort to Cowboy Bennett. The plastic chairs were painfully hard and the Holloway sisters demanded the old TV play only soap operas each afternoon. He was easy game for the nurses at pill time and somehow he was always running over the other residents' corns in his wheelchair.

But the lobby offered some refuge for Cowboy —at least it put distance between him and his roommate. Clyde Jenkins was eighty-five, rapidly declining in mind and body, and was convinced a moat ought to be constructed around the home to ward off rattlesnakes and Mexicans. He frequently awoke in the night and upset Cowboy by screaming that one or the other was about to get him.

Golden Shadows, a T-shaped, one-story structure of tan brick with a tar-and-gravel roof, sat on a dusty West Texas hill about a mile south of Sandero between the VFW and the rodeo grounds. It was home for about fifty-five aged. Two giant picture windows of the lobby faced west, for the afternoon sunshine. In the hot dry months of summer Cowboy often rolled his wheelchair to one of the windows and counted dust devils. Now, in the last days of autumn, long after the first frost, Cowboy would press closely to the window and search for cloudbanks building on the northwest horizon. When one was found, he immediately announced to all lobbymates:

"Well, looks like a norther's coming. Better get out your heavy garments."

Cowboy Bennett saw himself as a protector of Golden Shadows residents. He would not be living at the home except for the pickup accident three years ago. He drove a wheelchair now, had lost thirty pounds and he sometimes forgot exactly where he was, but he didn't consider these things major.

His daughter, Lisa, had urged him to move in from the ranch. She said with mother gone now he might fall down in a pasture and die before anyone would miss him. Fort Worth was nearly 200 miles away and she just couldn't be checking on him all the time. But Cowboy preferred to chance ending up buzzard bait in some remote pasture. He finally gave in only after Mrs. Walters, the home supervisor, persisted that she needed someone like him to help look after the other residents — and after she promised he could move in his old cowboy gear. His room was decorated with a mounted pair of silver spurs, a rigging from his last rodeo, a bridle with rotting reins. All he lacked was a saddle.

"Know why they call me Cowboy?" He was sitting in his wheelchair in the lobby one afternoon, speaking to Grandma McAllister. She ignored him. The only others in the lobby were the Holloway sisters, holding hands and monopolizing the TV. "I say, do you want to know why they call me Cowboy?"

Grandma McAllister remained silent. In her lap she clutched a small black purse that, according to rest home rumor, contained her life savings. She in some ways was luckier than Cowboy. Most of her kids lived nearby, but she refused to live with any of them. After breaking her hip she lived alone for years, and had no trouble getting around in her wheelchair. Twice the town marshal had to pick her up for blocking traffic on the square when she wheeled out under the blinking yellow light. One day she journeyed almost a mile west of Sandero to the interstate entrance ramp. That's when the kids gave her the ultimatum: us or the rest home.

"Well, I'll tell you anyway," Cowboy said. "There weren't no horse I couldn't break. When I was at the Flying W, ranchers came all the way from West Texas to get me to help out. They'd give me a corral full of wild broncs and I'd have them eating sugar outta my hand by noon. I used to ride in that big rodeo at Stamford, the Cowboy Reunion. They still remember me over there, lots of the old ones do."

Grandma McAllister reached down and pulled up one of her sagging nylons, paying no attention to Cowboy. He reminded her too much of her former husband, who ran off in the early '50s with a beautician he met at a rodeo dance. The only other men in her life were her five sons-in-law, four of them wife-beaters. The other had gout.

The Holloway sisters were meanwhile totally absorbed with "Our Daily Bread," an unfolding drama of a college girl who didn't want to come home for Christmas and tell her mother, infested with cancer, and her father, an alcoholic infidel, that she was pregnant by her colored boyfriend. The sisters were near tears.

"They brought an old bronc from somewhere up in the Rockies that'd never been ridden," Cowboy went on. "Name was Widow Maker. Mean as the dickens. You'd be getting down on him in the chute and he'd try to bite your fool leg off. See, he wanted to get you on the ground so he could stomp on your sideburns a little."

Cowboy laughed softly and rolled his chair closer to Grandma. He leaned forward. "Well, we exploded outta that chute, me and that crazy bronc, and he did the durndest to throw me off." Cowboy was all excitement. "I rode him. And I mean I didn't ride him a few seconds like today's cowboys do. I rode him around that arena nine-and-a-half minutes by the clock. You shoulda seen that saddle I won. I'd have it here but I lost it in a poker game to my brother-in-law. It's got All-Around Champion carved on it. Anyway the crowd went crazy when they saw I wasn't gonna get pitched off. I rode ole Widow Maker till he collapsed, and then I got off and—"

"Oh, Mr. Bennett. Mr. Bennett." A nurse had entered the lobby.

"And then after I got off—"

"Mr. Bennett, time to go. Have to get your chores done."

Grandma McAllister took a blue handkerchief edged with white lace from her purse. She blew her nose and wiped her forehead. Cowboy was disoriented; the story wasn't finished.

"Get all those toilets on the north wing and you'll be through for the day," the nurse said.

One of the Cowboy's responsibilities, along with changing the calendars and filling up the

Coke box, was visiting the north wing rooms twice a day to see the toilets were flushed. It was a health department safeguard against poor memory—not the most pride-building chore but Mrs. Walters said it was very important.

He rolled his chair into a hallway.

"Wilbur Bennett." It was Grandma McAllister, her voice as cold and cutting as a blue norther from the plains. Cowboy stopped his chair and spun it around. "I'm on to your tricks," she said, not looking at him.

Cowboy Bennett gazed at her and then turned around and rolled off.

"They're at it again," said the nurse back at the desk. "He's telling her that story about riding old Widow Maker. Today she's not even talking to him."

The others laughed. One of the younger nurses said, "Old people sure are something, aren't they?" Another nurse said wouldn't it be funny if Cowboy and Grandma McAllister got eyes for each other and started sparking on the sly. They might even get married. Somebody speculated on the sex life of geriatrics, to which the young nurse said get your mind out of the gutter.

"Oh, I wouldn't put nothing past these folks," asserted one of them. "Just last year we couldn't find Mr. Bennett one day. He'd disappeared from his room. Know where he was? In bed with old lady Martin. She's dead now. Anyway, all he had on was his boots and long underwear with the hatch open. She just had on her gown. I jerked back those sheets, and you should've seen them. They were giggling like two little kids playing doctor." The nurse paused and shook her head. "You can't put anything past these old people. They're more like kids than kids are. Watch them at the Christmas party. Believe you me, there's no place where Santa Claus is more alive than in the old folks' heads."

The next day a letter came for Cowboy. It was from his daughter, Lisa.

> *Dear Papa,*
>
> *Just to let you know you'll be receiving a big box in the next few days. Don't you dare open until Christmas. Bruce has a bar association banquet and looks like we won't get to come for the holidays. Be sure to eat all your meals and do what the nurses say. I'll call you Christmas Day. All my love, Lisa*
>
> *P.S. The gift should make you the hit of the home! Merry Xmas!*

Christmas. Cowboy had almost forgotten. It was scarcely a week away. And a big box was coming. This puzzled him. He rolled his chair closer to the window for better light and reread the letter.

A big box, he said again to himself. Hit of the home. What the devil might it be? His stomach quivered. Always before Lisa had been predictable about gifts. Boots three years ago, boots last year, white shirts two years ago. And always she asked what he wanted. How would she know what to get? She hadn't called in two months and hadn't visited since last summer, when—he suspected—she had really come to see how her mother's grave was being cared for. That visit was a bad one.

Cowboy was rooming with J. Grady Edwards, "Sr.," retired president of Sandero First National, who used to glide through the halls in his electric wheelchair telling everybody the mashed potatoes were better than laxatives. Cowboy and the old man were always fighting. Mr. Edwards had refused to let Lisa visit their room, so she and Cowboy were relegated to the lobby the entire visit, competing with television and the Holloway sisters. He was glad when J. Grady Edwards, Sr., and his electric wheelchair moved into the new nursing home in Abilene.

Cowboy suddenly stiffened in his chair and gripped the arms tightly as he leaned back. His heart beat mightily, as if he were easing down once again onto a wild horse. It had hit him. Of course. Lisa was giving him an electric wheelchair for Christmas. With three speeds, no doubt. She had commented how nice they must be when she saw old man Edwards. Cowboy flushed at how nice and tricky his daughter was.

"Say, Clyde," he called to his roommate, who was peeking out the other window toward one end of the parking lot. "Guess what I'm getting for Christmas."

"Shh," Clyde said with a finger to his lips. He had an old army blanket wrapped around him from head to foot. "I think they're coming," he whispered. "My God, they are. They're taking my parking place!"

"Who's coming, Clyde?"

Clyde moaned softly. "They got my spot."

"Clyde, you know you ain't got no parking spot. You ain't been sneaking a little nip with Harley Wilson again, have you? Listen, I wanna tell you what I'm getting for Christmas."

"Those Meskins," Clyde mumbled. "Now they're coming inside. Oh, Cowboy, what're we going to do?"

Cowboy looked into the parking lot. A battered '57 Chevy with reflector mud flaps and bumper stickers saying "God's Watching" and "Goat Ropers Need Love Too" had pulled into the lot. Catrina Valdez, a kitchen helper, was coming to work. "Don't worry yourself like that, Clyde. I once knew a bull rider who was a Meskin. Wiry little guy named Mendoza who could run faster and spit further than anybody I ever seen. He was real nice."

Clyde had his face pressed to the window to see where Catrina went. He looked over and said, "I read in the *Reporter-News* where they're causing trouble in the Abilene schools."

"Clyde, that was three years ago. They ain't even raised their hand to go to the bathroom since that bunch got thrown in the jug."

"They call themselves, CHEE-canos now," Clyde said, and shuddered. "They can really use them switchblades."

"You're right," Cowboy said, scratching himself. "They're coming across the parking lot. I'll have to take care of it. You get back in bed, Clyde. I'll take care of everything."

"I don't know what I'd do without you," Clyde said.

"You better keep that blanket on," said Cowboy, peering out the window. "Those clouds are really building in the north. We'll have a real spine-chiller blow through here tonight."

Clyde got back into bed and Cowboy started for the door. "Just what are you getting for Christmas?" Clyde called.

Cowboy smiled. "A three-speed electric wheelchair."

The Christmas party was the event of the year. Committees and subcommittees were formed. Everyone was given some duty, however slight. The Holloway sisters were in charge of entertainment. Sadie McDonald, a former cook at Truck City, headed the refreshments group.

Nellie Hawkins, the old local elementary art teacher, directed the decorations committee. Anyone bed-ridden or unspecialized would be put in Nellie's group, for the first step in making tree decorations required merely cutting construction paper in strips.

Cowboy was named director of transportation for the second time, which meant he had to make sure everyone got to the party. Fading memories required Cowboy to visit many rooms on the day of the party to remind residents. Even then many of them wouldn't show up until Cowboy personally came to lead them out of their rooms. Last year only old man Edwards missed. He locked himself in the toilet and wouldn't come out. This year Cowboy was after a perfect record. He prevailed upon Mr. Walters to see Grandma McAllister was named assistant director of transportation.

The Volunteer Fire Department of Sandero gave the home a Christmas tree. It was a perfectly shaped blue spruce from New Mexico nearly seven feet tall. The decorations committee encircled the tree with four strands of colored lights. Construction paper rings backdropped with miniature Christmas scenes hung delicately from long-needled limbs, along with two dozen red balls surviving from last year. Atop the tree was a cherubic little angel boy with tinfoil wings and a golden halo. The little angel, which Nellie had made, held a hymnal and his mouth was open as if singing, his eyes painted reverently shut. A yellow light blinked from behind.

At the last moment, Clyde Jenkins and Harley Wilson pitched on a box of foil icicles without Nellie's permission. She was so mad she resigned as committee chairman.

"Hells-bells," said Harley, "icicles make it look real."

"No icicles ever looked like that—it's gaudy —all droopy and tangled," said Nellie.

Clyde said, "Long as I knew you and your mama, you two never could take a joke."

"Don't you dare bring my dead mama into this."

Peace came when some of the residents told Nellie her Christmas angel was the prettiest they had ever seen. They pleaded for her to take her job back. "I'll think about it," she said.

As the two men left the lobby Harley said, "Whoever saw an angel with no eyes?"

On the morning of the 23rd, a large box was delivered to the lobby of the Golden Shadows Rest & Care Home. It was Cowboy's, wrapped in brown paper and secured with twine. Immediately there arose among residents much curiosity and speculation. It was a stereo, a TV, a lifetime supply of cowboy boots, a half-dozen cases of Coors. Velma Roberts said it could only be a giant ceramic Praying Hands, but Harley Wilson said it was a galvanized pan and water pump for the live-bait house.

Of course Cowboy knew, but he wasn't telling. And Clyde knew. And he only told Alta Mae Givens. By sundown the entire north and west wings knew Cowboy was getting a three-speed electric wheelchair. "All the way from Cowtown," it was said.

That evening Cowboy dressed up in his best white shirt with pearl button-snaps and went down to the lobby. A half-dozen residents were inspecting the sea of gifts beneath the tree, including Grandma McAllister. Cowboy rolled up beside her. "Ought to be a good party" he said.

Grandma grunted.

Cowboy thought maybe her hearing was failing and said, much louder. "They say this one will be the best yet. Those Holloway sisters got a actor coming over from the junior college to put on a drama. And I hear the home's kicking in presents this year. Nothing fancy but something."

Grandma felt the Christmas spirit growing within her. Her daughters were coming after her tomorrow after the party and she would see Santa Claus come for the grandkids. There would be a big turkey for dinner, which, unlike that of the rest home, wouldn't taste like it came out of a can. She looked at Cowboy and decided to be half decent. "Mr. Bennett," she finally said. "Why'd you get me on that committee of yours?"

The question, even her speaking, surprised Cowboy. He cleared his throat and nervously picked his nose. "I thought you'd be right for the job," he said. "It ain't everybody that's responsible these days. I mean, if you came by my room and said let's go to the party and I didn't want to go, I'd probably go anyways. You got the grit to influence people. I'd be afraid not to go." He looked down and grimaced. "I mean, I think anybody'd want to go to a party you was going to."

Grandma was chuckling to herself. Both of them knew she was a threat to his position. She could fill the Coke box if she cared to, and flush all the toilets, and nobody had to tell her when the clouds were coming and when to get out her heavy garments. Sometimes she thought she would like to challenge him to an arm-wrestling contest. They could do it in the dining room so everybody could see. But then she took no pleasure in such things as looking for cloudbanks building on the horizon. The home, she concluded, needed somebody like Cowboy, however distasteful he was at times. "Anyway," she said. "I just want to thank you. I cut so many decorations last year that I got arthritis in my thumb and it still ain't well."

"You're mighty welcome," he said.

They talked a long while that evening, mapping plans for who would get whom to the party. Grandma would go after the menfolk and Cowboy the women, the obstinate and the forgetful. They talked about how they got to the home and about their families. Grandma observed that she must have at least thirty kin living in the area but, save two or three, they only came to visit on Easter, Thanksgiving or Christmas.

"That's the one bad thing about Christmas," she said. "You feel a little guilty about the things you should've done for people during the year. Everybody feels bad for old people at Christmas. I tell you, it must of hit the Seventh Day before the Good Lord could figure out his plan for the old ones."

Cowboy said yes, he knew what she meant. But he didn't really. He had only a vague notion of what she was saying. In fact, he forgot her words almost as soon as she said them. But the gist of what he felt compelled him to tell a story. It was about one of his foremen many years back who eventually got a ranch of his own. "His name was Homer, and he was sixty years old and never been married. People was always getting on him about his bachelorhood and he always just said he didn't want to rush anything. Well, one day he picks up and leaves and don't come back. Six months later he turns up with this twenty-year-old Meskin wife. Them same people who was getting on him about not being married really hollered, especially the church groups. They were going to see he got kicked outta church, but they finally found out he didn't belong to no church anyway. They said it was the worst thang they ever saw, marrying someone that much younger. And her a Meskin. Well, they had seven kids and he was still digging his own post holes till his heart gave out a couple of years ago." He winked at Grandma. "And they say we old folks can't cut it."

She thought he was getting awfully fresh but let it pass.

Save the two of them the lobby was bare. It was getting late. The colored lights from the tree flickered eerily off the green walls and a gusty north wind howled about the windows. The cold front hit and another — already paralyzing the upper Panhandle with ice and snow — was due tomorrow. Grandma and Cowboy sat in silence for a while. Then she reached over and tugged his sleeve. "Good night, Cowboy." she said. "I'm so glad you didn't talk rodeos. I never could stand the smell. Or them dances."

Cowboy remained in the lobby. He wanted to take a last look at the box that contained his mechanical wizard. It was the only electric wheelchair in the home, probably in town. He savored the possibilities. He could help set up races, against time, from the dining room to the lobby. He could organize a caravan of wheelchairs on Sunday afternoons, all tied together like a train, to parade before visitors.

Then it occurred to him. What if the box contained no wheelchair? What if it were

Praying Hands or a live-bait house? He studied the box. It was laying flat, about three feet by three and well over a foot high. Collapsed just right it would be perfect for a chair. He picked up one end. It felt light at first, no heavier than a case of beer or one of his old saddles. But he knew the newer chairs were streamlined and much lighter these days, and the batteries never came with them. So this would be about right. But he was still unconvinced. He finally loosened the twine, stretched it to one side, and tore back the tape holding down the brown paper and red gift paper underneath.

There was lettering on the end of the box: Contains (I) ea. 220542 Rocking Horse, Red Deluxe. *Godamighty.* Then he noticed the box was battered somewhat and had been opened before. What a scare! Lisa had gotten one of the kids a rocking horse and saved the box for future use. There was a hole near the flap at the end. Cowboy could see inside and he made the hole a little larger with his finger. He felt seventy years younger, and guilty. He couldn't feel much in the hole at first except the crinkled newspaper — then something smooth, soft and smooth, like fabric or simulated leather, the kind they often use on the backs and seats of wheelchairs. Quickly he rendered the paper and twine intact.

Just before turning in that night, he picked up his mounted spurs from the dresser and, trying to remember when he last used them, spun the little spiked stars, again and again.

The Golden Shadows Christmas party commenced promptly at five in the afternoon, almost the same time the first snow-carrying norther of the year hit town. The flakes were small and dry-looking and skittered around the porch. Darkness came prematurely and it was bitter cold outside. To the credit of Cowboy and Grandma, attendance was 100 percent. The perfumed ladies came in their dresses of flowered print. They had rouged cheeks and permanents newly set by a fleet of beauticians who had descended on the home that morning. The men, with what hair there was slicked down by green Fitch, came in baggy dark suits and skinny ties. The party might not have gotten off to such a rousing start except for the thoughtfulness of Harley Wilson, whose brother, Elmer, operated County Line Liquors. A fifth of Smirnoff's vodka found its way to the punch bowl and, though it wasn't much, it was enough.

More than just the Holloway sisters developed wet eyes when the junior college actor read a condensed version of "A Christmas Carol." Cowboy was so moved he volunteered to meet Mr. Dickens in a dark alley. He felt nobody could have written about Scrooge's being so mean to a little crippled boy without being that mean himself. There was a near fight between Sadie McDonald and Old Lady Mashburn over who'd get the bows from the Christmas wrappings. Sadie vowed she'd pinch Old Lady Mashburn's head off but they were separated before she got the chance. Two old maids started kissing all the men, an unprecedented passion at Golden Shadows, and one of only two major setbacks for the men that evening. The other was Harley Wilson. Harley, who had stationed himself at the punch bowl for refill duty, suddenly took ill and toppled into the Christmas tree. They had to rush him to the bathroom. The residents said it was the Asian flu, but the nurses suspected the punch. The tree survived.

Then came the opening of gifts. Mrs. Walters called names, and shaking hands plunged into work. The men ripped at the packages while the women cautiously picked at them so as not to disturb wrapping or bow. The home gave the women knitting kits and the men bow ties.

It was understood that Cowboy's box would be the last opened. As he lifted one end of the box with Grandma McAllister's help, the residents began to whisper. Realizing he was the center of attention, he suddenly looked up and said: "Y'all look here at Grandma. Don't she look purty? Smell that perfume? She smells ten times better than the best sheep dip I ever smelt." Everybody laughed, including Grandma, but she didn't laugh very much.

"I ain't got no idea what this thang could be," Cowboy said pulling off the last of the paper. "Well, looky here. Says here on the box I'm getting a rocking horse!" After the laughter died, he opened the card taped on the end of the box. The front of the card showed a man on horseback in a snow-covered field, pulling a big evergreen from the woods with his rope. In the background was a little white frame building with belfry and holly in the windows, and there was a light glowing inside and smoke puffing from the chimney, and someone was standing in the doorway, waiting. The scene jarred Cowboy, but his memory focused no more clearly than a too-distant station on his old crystal set, barely here one moment, then faded away forever. There was a note inside:

Hope you like this little surprise, Papa. Mrs. Walters said it would be okay for you to have it. Uncle Ted was real nice about it. Merry, Merry Xmas. Sorry I can't be there. Don't forget, I'll call. Love Lisa

Then Cowboy, in the happiest moment he could remember, opened the box.

They were stunned at first, all of them. Finally Clyde Jenkins said, "Boy howdy, a horse saddle. We got us a regular cowboy museum now."

And then everybody crowded around with oohs and ahs and ain't that nice and where're you going to put it?

"Gonna hang it from the ceiling and charge a nickel a peek?" Clyde asked.

Cowboy was shaking his head and grinning. His mouth was dry and he didn't know what to say. So it wasn't the three-speed wheelchair, but by George, they'd all have to believe him now, about him and old Widow Maker.

"Look," somebody said, "Got All-Around Champion—1927 carved on it."

Cowboy looked at Grandma for approval. "That's real nice, Cowboy. Real nice." Then she spun her chair around. "I gotta go see how Harley Wilson's doing. Poor thang."

The snow turned out to be a heavy one, wet and sticky, and it was to make this Christmas whiter than any in recent years. Cowboy sat up late in his room after the party and watched the gentle whiteness settle on the windowsill and fields beyond. The home was quiet. Clyde and the old army blanket were securely entangled, and he was asleep. Cowboy felt awfully tired inside, and thought maybe the day had been too much. He was cold and began rubbing his arms, now bony and loose of flesh, no longer full of "sin and sinew" as his daughter use l to say. He looked down to the shadowed heap on the floor, remains of the big box. Then he was startled.

"Why Mr. Bennett," a nurse said. "What are you doing still up? You shouldn't be staying up this late, not after a day like you had. Am I going to have to give you a pill?"

Cowboy didn't answer.

The nurse looked around the room. "I hear you're going to make this an Old West museum and charge admission. I think a nickel's too cheap. You could run them through here a quarter a head on Sunday afternoons." She couldn't tell if he was listening but continued anyway. "I don't guess I ever saw a real championship saddle before. You know, one that belonged to a champion cowboy from the old days."

Cowboy hesitated. "Never saw one?"

"Nope, never did."

"Never even been to a real rodeo, I'll bet," Cowboy said.

"Not exactly, but I did see a donkey baseball game down at the ballpark. People were getting throwed off all the time."

Oh Christ Godamighty, Cowboy thought.

"Those donkeys just scared the daylights out of me," the nurse said. "If one of them kicked you in the head it'd hurt as bad as a bronco, wouldn't it, Mr. Bennett?"

"Probably would," Cowboy said. "Course you know that they didn't used to worry about having arenas filled with sand, so you'd have a soft place to land."

"My, my," the nurse said. "You really had to be a man to want to rodeo in the old days."

Cowboy, feeling sprightly, said, "That's what a lotta folks say." They both were looking at the saddle in the corner, completely refurbished, eternal token to the conquest of old Widow Maker. Cowboy noticed the nurse smelled nice. A new hairdo, he supposed. He liked her. He could tell she was really interested in the rodeo.

"Here, take this," the nurse said, holding a pill and a little paper cup before him.

Cowboy looked at the pill and the cup, barely discernible in the faint light, and at the smooth arm extended. Suddenly he grabbed her wrist, knocking pill and cup to the floor, and quickly pressed his toothless mouth to her arm. The nurse was frightened, thinking Cowboy was mad about the pill and trying to bite her. "Mr. Bennett! Mr. Bennett! Stop it! Stop it I say!" But Cowboy held on, as determined as he would have been with a wilder creature in another time. And he was not biting. It was, as the nurse would tell the others at the desk, the wettest old gummy kiss you ever saw. ⁕

Reprinted with permission of The Ohio Journal

A Treasured Christmas Gift

By Frank Perkins

Frank Perkins, a native of Fort Worth, a Texas Christian University graduate and a longtime newsman in North Texas, died in 2004. He won a Sigma Delta Chi award for his coverage of the Kennedy assassination as a television reporter for WBAP, now KXAS/ Channel 5, and moved on to become a reporter, assistant state editor and military columnist at the Fort Worth Star-Telegram. *For the latter, he drew on his years in active and reserve Army service, in which he rose to the rank of lieutenant colonel. In this story, first published in the* Star-Telegram *on Christmas Day 1992, Perkins channels a city kid's country Christmas memory, revealing a quiet but vivid portrait of a quintessential Texas figure, a man who says little but sees much.*

I can still feel my most memorable Christmas gift in my hands, even though the gift was given to me decades and decades ago.

It was not fancy, nor expensive, nor wrapped in luxurious paper and bows. Instead, it was given as if it were my right to have it, and that made it even more special to me.

The gift was given by my stepgrandfather, a man whom I regarded with a mixture of puzzlement and awe and who I thought considered me of no consequence whatever.

It was 1946. The war was over and my father had returned safely from the U.S. Navy. It was

43

Christmas Eve, as usual, we would spend it and Christmas Day with my stepmother's parents in their small sharecropper's farmhouse in Denton County, between Little Elm and Frisco.

I was 12. The awkward age between childhood and the teen years. This particular Christmas, I especially felt the awkwardness. I was still too young to be included in my dad and stepuncle's Christmas Eve quail hunt that had become a family tradition.

I was too old to gather with my stepmother, her sisters and my stepgrandmother in the kitchen and peel potatoes and carrots and listen to the gossip and wisecracks that crackled like summer lightning from this remarkably verbal group.

"Get out from under our feet, boy, go find something to read or to do outside," my stepmother said to me as I hung around the small kitchen, already crowded with just my stepmother, her mother and two sisters.

A third sister and her husband would be coming that night after getting off work in Dallas.

There was nothing to do outside. I already had read everything in the small house, including the quaint *Farmer's Almanac*. There was no one my age, no neighbor kids, just a North Texas blackland farm in dead of winter, with a cold rain blowing down from the north over the small forgotten cemetery on a hill just north of the house. The temperature was dropping from the already chilly 40 degrees. I went out anyway and headed for the barn.

In the barn were a pair of mules, a wagon and my stepgrandfather, a tall, spare, monosyllabic man who had spoken perhaps 50 words to me since I entered his family in 1939 when my widowed dad married his youngest daughter. She had nursed him back to health after the car wreck that widowed him and left him with a year-old baby to raise.

The old man called my dad and his other in-laws by name, but he never called me anything but "boy."

He was engaged in one of his favorite chores, grooming his two fine Missouri mules, his most prized possessions and in the opinion of the whittlers and spitters at Dick Riddle's General Store in Little Elm, the finest pair of mules in Denton County.

The mules stood quietly as he moved between them in the straw-filled stable, brushing their mouse-grey coats to a satiny sheen with a curry comb; rubbing their velvety noses and scratching behind those long, expressive ears.

He was thin and to me, mysterious. His clear blue eyes were friendly, but a sweeping white mustache, the tips stained by the tobacco he chewed, and his silence made him a figure of awe. Like the other members of his family, I called him "Our Papa."

In the summer, when I made extended visits to the farm, I would ride with him for hours on a plow pulled by those mules.

It was a fantastic, yet strangely speechless experience. The clean-animal smell of the warm mules, the creaking of the harness as they shouldered the plow through the rich black land; nests of baby mice dug up by the plow blade, rabbits wheeling away in flight almost from under the mules' hooves.

None of these things were everyday events to me; they did not occur in the sophistication of Fort Worth.

Despite all these wonders, he spoke not a word, although I would yell and point and shout, "Look, Our Papa, a rabbit!" I would turn and see only a small smile under his tobacco-stained mustache. Then he would acknowledge my attempt to share with him what I thought was a wondrous occurrence with a slight nod.

When he would spy something interesting I had missed, he would click his tongue in a softer sound than the whiplike snap he used when he was starting his mules.

Hearing the click, I knew he had something important to reveal and would look at him. He would raise a finger and point and I would follow the line of the finger and see another wondrous sight such as a neighbor's mare with her newborn foal or a huge red-tailed hawk sitting on a distant fence post.

I thought he was a remarkable man because of his silence. He would sit in his favorite rocker in front of the Christmas tree, his presents neatly stacked nearby, while his sons, daughters, daughters-in-law and grandchildren all talked, laughed, joked and jabbered at the top of their lungs because my stepgrandmother, Our Mama, was as deaf as a post.

Through all that loud, raucous fun, he would sit and smile, his eyes dancing, and say not a word. A particularly barbed sally would draw a short "Ha" from him.

But now it was supper time on Christmas Eve so he put up the curry comb, and he and I wordlessly walked back from the barn into that warm kitchen for a supper of chicken-fried steak, gravy, mashed potatoes, preserved corn, pickled beets and hot biscuits.

Outside, the first ice began to form on the mud-slicked back roads as the temperature continued to fall. In the living room, my stepmother and her sisters kept up their gossiping while Our Papa read the newspaper and Our Mama fussed about what was keeping Aunt Eula and Uncle Clarence. We all decided it was that darned old Dallas traffic.

I remember going to bed and to sleep amid the murmur of those voices and the chiming of the old Seth Thomas clock on the mantel.

Three hours later, at midnight, the old man was shaking me gently.

"Get up, boy. I need your help. Dress warm and get a heavy coat," and then he was gone.

Wonderingly, because those were the longest three sentences he had ever spoken to me, I got up, pulled on my warmest clothes and a new fleece-lined leather jacket and went into the kitchen.

The women were all there, sitting around the table in their robes and housecoats. A pot of coffee boiled on the stove.

"A neighbor came by and told us Aunt Eula and Uncle Clarence ran off the iced-up road up by the store," one of them explained. "Our Papa wants you to go with him in the wagon to get them."

About that time I heard the jingling of the mules' harnesses and went outside and climbed up beside the old man, bundled in a shapeless mackinaw on the wagon seat. He gave that special "giddyap" click of his tongue and we were off into the chillingly cold, dark night.

The icy ground cracked and crunched under the iron-rimmed wheels of the wagon as we negotiated the turn onto the Frisco road and headed toward the store, about two miles away.

Once the mules were lined out straight, there came my special little click from his lips. I looked over at him and he suddenly pushed the reins at me.

"Here," he said. "You drive 'em."

Amazed and wondering, I took the reins. It was like grabbing electricity. The power of the mules slugging into their harness pulled me to my feet and thrilled me to my core. Our Papa grabbed the tail of my new jacket and pulled me back into the seat. "Stay with 'em, boy," he said.

By then the mules had figured out something was haywire. Even in the blackness I could see those remarkably expressive ears whipping back and forth, semaphoring confusion and question about who had the reins.

The reins sagged a bit in my hand, that awful pull easing. Then came that whipcrack tongue click of his followed by a rare "Hi, mules!" from Our Papa. Instantly, the four ears snapped into the "alert" position and that awe-inspiring pull came back through the reins as they moved back into the harness and resumed their easy gaits.

I have never again had such a sense of power, or connection with the basic elements of that earth as I did at that moment. This was what men did. This was what being a man was all about; controlling intelligent, loyal beasts and moving to the rescue of your family in the dark of night.

Heady stuff. And I was being allowed a taste of it. The veil of the mysteries of adulthood had been pulled aside a bit.

And suddenly there was Aunt Eula and Uncle Clarence's 1939 Ford V-8, its streamlined nose buried in the ditch.

I pulled back on the reins and then died a thousand deaths as my voice cracked when I called out, "Whoa-a-a-a, mules!" There followed another semaphoring of mule ears at the strange screech and the rather tentative tug on the reins, but they stopped.

My stepaunt and uncle, carrying their Christmas gifts, quickly climbed aboard the wagon and bundled in blankets and quilts sent by the women.

Then my stepgrandfather turned to me and said, "Get us home, boy."

I imitated his tongue click. It was a poor effort, but the ears wavered a time or two and then the beasts surged into the harness and we were moving toward the store a mile or so away where we could turn without risk of sliding off the now-deep frozen ruts into the ditch.

I was terrified about the turn. How did you do it? Then I remembered Our Papa's gnarled hands and how they worked to make those turns while plowing.

At the appointed time, I began the drill. It was almost too much for my aunt. She had already had the unsettling experience of winding up in a ditch that night and she wasn't quite up to sitting idly by while a nervous 12-year-old soloed at turning a wagon and two-mule hitch.

She stood up in the rear of the wagon and reached toward the reins. I was concentrating on the turn and was unaware of what was going on until the old man said in the sharpest tone I had ever heard him use: "Sit down, Eula."

Eula sat down.

A half-hour later we were back home and Eula was chattering away with her sisters and mother. Clarence had carried in the luggage and the gifts and the old man and I were unharnessing the mules: the first time I had ever been allowed to help with that chore.

My hands were still tingling with the feel of the vitality and power of those animals, transmitted back to me through those worn and patched leather reins.

We spent 10 more minutes wiping down the mules and then returned to the house where a still-jabbering family, now joined by my dad and other stepuncles back from the quail hunt, waited.

As we stepped up on the back porch, the old man put his hand on my shoulder and called me by my name for the first time.

"Good work, Frank."

That hour in a freezing open wagon, being given the responsibility for driving the finest pair of mules in Denton County to rescue relatives in need, was the finest Christmas gift anyone has ever given me. ♥

Reprinted with permission of the Fort Worth Star-Telegram

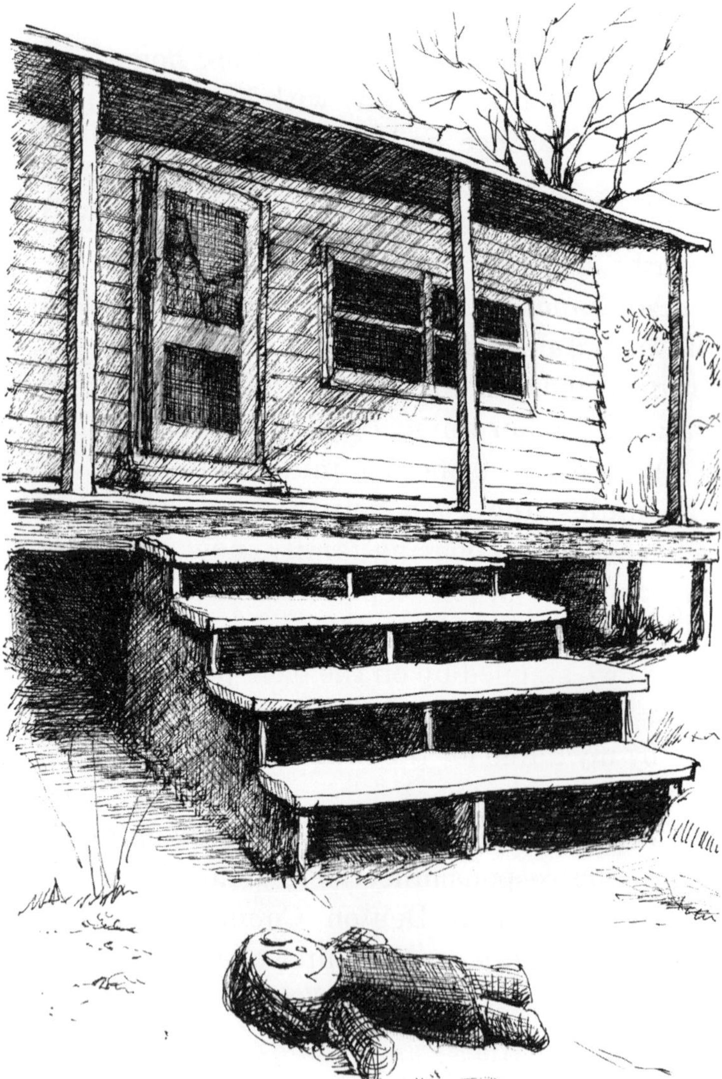

The Doll

By Jerry Flemmons

This 1967 story, honored as best feature story of the year by the Headliners Club of Austin, became one of the Fort Worth Star-Telegram's *most reprinted and anthologized articles. Flemmons later expanded it into a longer story, but this is the form it originally took. Flemmons is a Fort Worth legend, having reported for the* Star-Telegram *for some three decades and written several books. When the native Texan died in 1999, a colleague eulogized him by saying: "Some readers preferred his columns ... Some liked* Texas Siftings, *for years a monthly celebration of all things Texan ... But most of us just liked anything with his name on top. Grocery list or bail bond application — if Jerry's hand touched it, you read it."*

Roy died a long time ago, and there is no one to remember him. He had no friends and probably no family and was not the kind of person about whom anyone would reminisce. People in the small East Texas town said only of Roy that he was "the most useless man in the county." I suppose he was. Roy — his full name was Roy William Simpson — never held a job or did anything that could be considered steady work. His only pastime was drinking. He consumed whiskey and cheap wine in awesome amounts if he could obtain either, though usually he could not. More often he drank aftershave lotion, hair oil, various cooking extracts and other everyday, ordinary liquids no one but Roy considered alcoholic.

Roy existed by stealing. He stole vegetables from gardens and nearby farms. He stole from old man Otis Adams' egg farm, though he never took chickens, which would have made Otis angry enough to call the sheriff. He stole only eggs, and old man Adams would joke about Roy's thievery to the men gathered at the filling station — "Roy can steal an egg 'fore it's laid," he claimed. The loafers would laugh uproariously at the thieving ways of the county's most useless citizen.

Once, between vegetable seasons, Otis' chickens quit laying for some reason, and Roy was forced to steal Mrs. Truax's registered poodle. He perhaps intended selling the scrawny little dog for money with which to buy his distilled liquors or vanilla extract. The sheriff caught him and returned the poodle to Mrs. Truax. Roy was not arrested. He was never arrested for his thefts. Townspeople, in fact, rarely complained of Roy's stealing. He was just an irritating cross they bore, like mosquitoes in the spring and a poor cotton crop.

Somewhere in Roy's background was a term in prison, probably endured for the theft of something more valuable than vegetables, eggs or poodles. He rarely spoke of his jail days, but he told me prison was not oppressive except that he suffered from a lack of alcohol. He had worked for a time in the penitentiary's license plate shop and later transferred to the laundry, where he washed sheets and stitched up rips in mattress ticking.

Aside from stealing, Roy's source of income was a sad and cruel game. He was the object of ridicule for local teenagers and filing-station loafers. The kids would say, "Bet you a quarter you can't run up to the cafe and back in 30 seconds." Roy could not and knew he could not, but he always tried. The quarter was his for playing the fool. He would start off in a kind of shuffling trot, pumping his arms in awkward rhythm, like a man going nowhere. The kids would laugh and point at Roy and run alongside taunting him.

Adult loafers were no less cruel. One would say, "Roy, can you dance a jig? Betcha four bits you can't." Roy would try. Or he would pat his head and rub his stomach for a dime. The teenagers and adults never seemed to tire of the sad sport. Perhaps it was their unconscious way of supporting a tired, frail, useless, liquorruined old man.

Roy had no status at all in the small town except that of cooperating buffoon. He could not even claim the title of town drunkard.

That honor belonged to the local bootlegger who drank more than he sold. That sot, according to townspeople, had a regular, albeit illegal, occupation; Roy was unemployed. The bootlegger got Roy's money when he had any. If not, Roy knocked politely at the rear door of the general store and Mr. Ferris would hand out a bottle of extract. There was an unpopular bond between Roy and Mr. Ferris, and the storekeeper was criticized by the church people for giving Roy the alcoholic extracts. But Mr. Ferris took a drink now and then, and he laughed off the complaints from the town's more sober citizens. He continued to pass bottles out the back door to Roy. Mr. Ferris liked the old man. One Christmas he gave Roy a plaid scarf, and Roy wore it like a regal ascot tie under his faded jacket.

The cruel pranks brought Roy a couple of dollars a week. Twice a year he received an envelope with a $10 bill in it. Most people speculated the letters came from a son or daughter, but no one knew for sure. At those times he bought bottles of whiskey or gin and stayed drunk for days. It mostly was after the $10 bills arrived that Roy was drunk on Main Street and people would tsktsk and complain that he was the most useless man in the county.

Because Roy performed for the jokers, they thought him not quite bright, and perhaps he was not. Only rarely did he contribute more than a word or two in a conversation. But Roy was clever enough to live by the community's charity without a shred of shame, and that requires some intelligence.

Roy was a man of some years when I saw him, perhaps 55 or 56. His exact age was impossible to determine because liquor and poor diet long before had wrinkled Roy's body until his 130 pounds seem bounded inside a smoked sausage sack. I remember his voice as something unreal, gravely and hoarse and lowpitched, the scratchy sound of cheap whiskey. His eyes were the color of stained copper, like old pennies, and his nose was too large for his face. I never saw him when he was not wearing the same clothes. His wardrobe did not change, winter or summer. Roy wore dirty dark-green corduroy pants, oncebrown shoes with thin heels, a bluish work shirt and an ancient Eisenhower Army jacket. The scarf given him by Mr. Ferris, red and green Scotch plaid, either hung straight under his jacket or was crossed in the continental style. The jacket's regular buttons had been lost, and Roy had replaced them with bright-yellow plastic buttons. The yellow buttons only made Roy seem more of a fool.

For years, Roy slept on a dirty, faded rug in the tool shed behind the cotton gin. When the area's cotton crop declined and the gin was torn down, he moved to an abandoned sharecroppers' shack two miles south of town, on land owned by the bank. He boarded up windows and stuffed newspapers into cracks. For a stove he used a rickety icebox lined with asbestos shingles. Roy took his rug, his only possession, and continued sleeping on it.

The September before the winter in which Roy died, the community suffered a tragedy. Tragedy is the soul of small towns because one person's misfortune becomes public property. Tragedy assumes a collective face and the sorrow is borne by all. At least, that's what happened in Roy's town.

Margaret Lee was not a pretty child. She was 5, perhaps 6, with straight blonde hair the color of cobwebs and watery blue, almost icy, eyes. She was thin, and her skin was sickly white. The only time I ever saw her, she wore a little girl's print dress and carried a battered rag doll across the crook of her left arm. Margaret Lee and her mother lived a block south of the filling station in a threeroom frame house. The mother was plain, too, and bigboned, a large woman with a worn face. She came from Austria and spoke English with a halting, heavy accent.

Margaret's father had met and married the woman while stationed in Europe as an Army corporal. He brought her home to America, to the small East Texas town. The child was 4 when her father burned to death in the gasoline truck accident on a lonely Kansas road. Mother and daughter lived on the little insurance money left by the father's death. The mother baked pies and cakes for additional income.

In late summer, doctors confirmed Margaret Lee had leukemia.

Unable to save the little girl's life, they set about the tedious work of prolonging it. The mother was almost insane with grief and cried hysterically when neighbors came to visit. The community gathered itself to help Margaret Lee. Each church held special collections for the child. Baptists beat Methodists, but Methodist women took turns driving Margaret Lee and her mother to the county seat hospital, and that charity was said to have balanced the smaller monetary contribution. The Lions arranged for a bloodmobile to come one Saturday and park on the empty lot next to Mr. Ferris' store.

Townspeople donated blood for the child.

One of the pranksters brought Roy to the line and said, "Betcha six bits they won't take your blood, Roy." The old man stood his turn, but when the doctors saw the bland eyes, the alcoholic sheen of Roy's skin and his dirty beard and smelled his unwashed body covered by the Army jacket with clownish yellow plastic buttons, they sent him away. Roy collected his 75 cents and got drunk in the alley behind Mr. Ferris' store.

A month before Christmas, Margaret Lee let it be known she wanted to see her grandfather. The mother did not beg, but she asked if it would be possible to raise enough money to bring the Old World grandfather from Austria to the East

Texas town to see the granddaughter he had never met and who soon would die. Again the churches took collections. Mr. Ferris donated a day's receipts, and even Old Man Adams contributed his egg money. Someone asked Roy for a $2 donation, and the loafers laughed when he snorted and stamped away.

Margaret Lee became weaker. Her mother argued with doctors who wanted to hospitalize the girl. The mother asked to keep Margaret Lee home until the grandfather arrived. So the Methodist women continued their weekly drives to the county seat hospital for Margaret Lee's treatments. More than a week before Christmas, the letter containing airfare and expense money was sent to the small Austrian village.

The next day Margaret Lee lost her rag doll.

The Methodist lady whose turn it was to drive Margaret Lee to the hospital thought the doll had been left in the waiting room. Perhaps it was, but the doll could not be found when they returned to search.

So began another round of charity by the churchwomen. Dozens of rag dolls were delivered to Margaret, some storebought, some homemade. The child rejected each and every one of them. None, she cried, was her rag doll. Her father had given the doll to her. That was the difference, explained the mother. Margaret Lee, pale and nervous and weak, announced that Santa Claus would return the doll.

Christmas approached, and the town prepared to make the holiday the happiest ever for the little girl. They bought most of the smaller toys in Mr. Ferris' store and made trips to the county seat for larger games and mechanical contraptions.

On December 23, Roy received one of his $10 envelopes and immediately bought a supply of whiskey and gin. He struck out across the blackland fields, and no one ever saw him alive again.

The tragedy of Margaret Lee brought the town together as nothing before, and although she was cranky and whiny about the loss of her doll, Margaret Lee's last Christmas was splendid.

There was a momentary rush of concern when Margaret Lee had to be taken to the hospital for more blood on the day before Christmas. She returned and was put to bed. A Lions Club member volunteered his pickup, and toys were collected from homes and delivered to Margaret Lee's house at 10 p.m. on Christmas Eve. Before she slept that night, she talked about the doll Santa would return to her and about the grandfather who would come in a day or two.

Christmas morning there were rag dolls, dozens of them. Big ones and small ones, dolls with happy faces and dolls with sad faces, boy dolls and girl dolls, dolls dressed in every conceivable costume, some in bright colors, others in patterned clothes. But not one of them was Margaret Lee's doll, and she cried as she opened each package, only to find another, different doll. The mother held the child to comfort her. The rest of the day she played listlessly with her new toys and the unwanted rag dolls as she lay in bed.

Late Christmas day, the snow began, huge uncommon flakes for that season in East Texas. Margaret Lee and her mother watched the snow from a front window and talked about the grandfather. Snow had covered the ground and lay in drifts around the house as darkness came.

I never saw the grandfather, but people said he was a small man with a gray mustache and spoke no English. The grandfather and Margaret Lee visited for a day. Then an ambulance came and took the child to the hospital. Snow stayed on the ground for two days before melting. The weather remained unseasonably cold early in January, and snow came again, not as heavily, but the ground disappeared once more under the layer of white. Late in January, two rabbit hunters found Roy's body.

Roy lay under a small oak tree in the center of a field midway between the town and his shack. An empty whiskey bottle was beside him. The sheriff said there was no mistaking who it was. Roy was not wearing his Army jacket or the plaid scarf, but the corduroy pants were his, and the scuffed brown shoes with worn heels, so the sheriff identified the body that way. He had died from cold and exposure.

People said Roy, in death, was as dumb and drunk as he was in life; he should never have gone into the freezing weather, they said, without his heavy clothes.

Roy was buried in the cemetery behind the Methodist Church, off in a corner, with the county paying funeral expenses. Sober folks saw Roy's cold death as retribution for a wasted whiskeyfilled life, and no one seemed to care very much that the county's most useless man was gone.

Margaret Lee died in midJanuary with her grandfather at her bedside. Her funeral brought out most of the town's population. Mr. Ferris closed his store, and even the loafers left the filling station long enough to watch Margaret Lee buried on a cold winter day beneath a gray distant sky.

The mother sold the frame house, and she and the grandfather left the little town and returned to Austria.

Almost a month passed before I heard about Margaret Lee's rag doll. Mr. Ferris said she had had the doll when the ambulance came to take her to the hospital for the last time, and he thought it was the doll she had lost. Later, when he looked at it more closely, he knew, and he asked the mother about it.

Christmas Day, an hour after dark, when the snow had stopped, the mother had heard a noise on the front porch. She opened the door. The mother saw no one, but the rag doll lay in the snow, next to the steps.

Margaret Lee, the mother said, loved the doll on sight. It was a pitiful thing, ugly and poorly made, but Margaret Lee said that if Santa could not find her doll he knew the kind of doll she wanted. She loved the doll and cuddled it to her as she lay dying in the hospital.

Mr. Ferris said the doll was like the old one, ragged and worn and lumpy. It had, he said, red and green Scotch plaid skin and, for eyes, two bright-yellow plastic buttons. 🙂

Reprinted with permission of the Fort Worth Star-Telegram

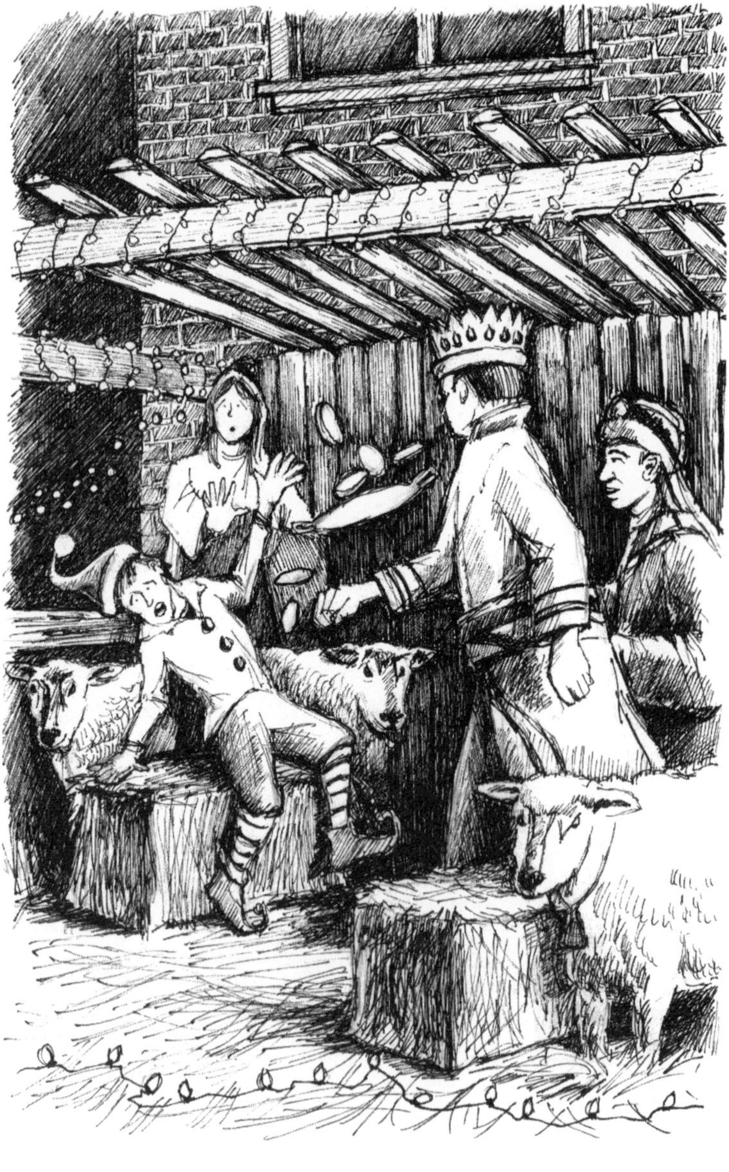

The Night the Wise Man Sucker-Punched the Elf

By Mike Blackman

Here's how Baylor journalism professor and former Fort Worth Star-Telegram executive editor Mike Blackman recalls writing his 1997 tale of small-town vendettas, poultrycide, lost love at the Dairy Queen and all-around merry mayhem during the goodwill-to-men season: "One day Lisa Davis, then one of our Star-Telegram features editors, showed up in my office and asked if I could do some kind of Christmas story for her section — they needed one to fill space. I told her I could probably think of something — when's deadline? Tomorrow, she said. That's when I told her I'd have to make something up."

They had been rivals for more than 30 years, Donnie and Eddie Lee, and now they were poised for their grandest tussle yet: Who would win Best Christmas Yard Display of Funston City.

So grand were their next-door displays, a special committee was imported from Abilene to ensure impartial judging. Not only would the winner receive $500 in gift certificates from local merchants, but a photo of the winning yard would be submitted for publication in newspapers around the state.

The excitement over the contest had grown steadily, since Donnie moved back to Funston

City and Eddie Lee more or less found God. At first, their yard scenes were relatively modest affairs, a few fiberglass reindeer gracing Donnie's yard, with a chimney-bound Santa, sack over shoulder, trekking atop the roof; and in Eddie Lee's yard, a homemade, hand-painted Nativity that featured a Baby Jesus with the most fetching blue eyes.

Each year thereafter, Donnie and Eddie Lee tried to one-up each other, and the displays snowballed in complexity and imagination. Now, this year, "It looks like the Macy's Parade ran smack dab into Monkey Ward's toy department," marveled the mayor of Funston City.

The local weekly would observe in a front-page editorial:

> *Our town is doubly blessed with the creative brilliance of two of our most prominent citizens, Mr. Donald Trappers and Mr. Eddie Lee Madley, who demonstrate so dramatically the rich reward of competition and free enterprise. Where else in West Texas would you see a full acre of Santa's workshop on such a heroic scale—imagine a 2-story Santa and 8-foot elves! And right next door, the story of Baby Jesus told in more than 30,000 lights beaming across the front lawn, straight from the Gospel itself! And that's just a fraction of their efforts!*

True, there was much more this year. Donnie rented a miniature train from Fort Worth to ride the kids through his Santa Land, whistle-tooting along the way, while Eddie Lee hired members of the high school drama club for minimum wage—all the caramel popcorn balls they could eat—to stage a live Nativity scene. So authentically detailed was the Nativity creation that not only did it feature a live Baby Jesus, but homecoming queen Dorothy Dixon, voted most untouchable by the football team, was cast as the Virgin Mary. Three Wise Men came bearing genuine frankincense and myrrh in gold-glittered Dixie Cups.

"It is so real and lifelike you'd swear you were in the Holy Land," the weekly Funston City Star further opined.

Donnie—he and the wife presided over his production attired as Santa and Mrs. Claus—dressed all his naked mesquite trees in twinkly red lights, and lit his front hedges in green and red, spelling out "Holiday Cheers!," and decorated the two big cedars guarding his front door in 2-foot fluorescent candy canes. He hired a fleet of junior high elves to serve hot chocolate and sugar cookies to passing motorists.

Eddie Lee, in his decorations, just a hundred feet away over a tall brick fence, stationed eight papier-mâché reindeer and a plastic longhorn bull upon his multigabled roof (Rudolphs done sold out). For his ever-growing Nativity scene, he installed from his farm three live lambs, two old buffaloes and an indignant donkey named Saul, plus a billy goat and Lucy, a goose. No pigs.

"I like realism," Eddie Lee said. "They don't eat pork, you know."

To each side and over his house, Eddie Lee erected his newest, proudest creation—two towering crosses, outlined in red 60-watt bulbs, and strung between the crosses the words ON EARTH PEACE, some 8 feet high, sparkling in blue lights racing in procession, right to left, like they were chasing one another. Ah, his pièce de résistance. Eddie Lee earnestly believed his ON EARTH PEACE display would make him a winner this year, finally. The high school art teacher was particularly impressed with the inverted wording, saying it symbolized an appreciation for Christmases traditional. In reality, Eddie Lee had plugged in the transformers backward.

Judging was scheduled the Sunday night before Christmas.

Yes, everybody said, these remarkable Christmas displays were truly a work of heart, and put their little town on the economic development map, especially after the Abilene paper did a story about "the Christmas displays so astonishing that even Ripley wouldn't believe it."

Nightly, hundreds of folks from all surrounding counties, cars packed with pillows and kids in footed pajamas, made the pilgrimage, so many, in fact, the police auxiliary had to be called out. Cars backed up two full miles, headlights glowing like Broadway gone country. One neighbor provided valet service, three bucks a car, for those who wished to linger.

The little town, 80 miles from the nearest interstate, finally had something to cheer about besides its sorry football team—that being a prolific export of Christmas cheeseburgers and unleaded gas. Some folks said all this publicity might help the town attract one of those new state prisons.

One morning, a couple weeks or so before Christmas, something strange happened. Lucy the goose was found dead in the manger, and, from the position of the body, wrapped in an old hooded sweatshirt, police said it looked like foul play.

"Her little neck was snapped almost clear around. Big knot on her head, too. Big as a duck egg," said Police Chief Dim Whittleton. "Looks like somebody had a score to settle."

Eddie Lee was beside himself. "Lucy was family—for years—my little girl's favorite, when she came to visit," he told the chief. "He'll pay for this—he dang sure will, Lord as my witness." He waved his hand toward the house next door, Donnie's house.

Pressed for details, Eddie Lee said: "I ain't saying nothing else."

When police moved their investigation next door, Donnie adamantly denied culpability in Lucy's demise.

"Look," he said, "Eddie Lee's blamed me for everything but El Nino since his first divorce. We haven't spoken more than a dozen words the last 20 years. I'm sorry he can't seem to get on with life. I know he's a good man, but I consider this unwarranted harassment, if not slander. Should I get a good lawyer, Chief?"

"No, that won't be necessary," the chief said. "But don't leave town."

That night, all the Nativity personnel were saddened, especially the shepherds. Lucy's death was on everyone's lips. Who would do such a thing?

"There is a cold-blooded killer loose, walking among us," suggested one of the angels. "And somebody knows something." She looked suspiciously at her colleagues, each one of them.

When some of the sugar-cookie elves from next door came to pay their respects, a Nativity angel interpreted one of the elves' condolences as slightly less than sincere, and there commenced a disagreement, which rapidly deteriorated when one of the gift-bearing Wise Men sucker-punched the littlest cookie elf, who tripped backward over a bale of hay and gave up all his cookies to three hungry, if delighted, sheep. Only the collective pleadings of Joseph and Mary, joined by Mrs. Santa Claus, Donnie's wife, who witnessed the commotion from her bedroom window and came running, prevented an unencumbered melee. Somebody called the police, but the cookie elf, still woozy, could not identify his assailant.

"Had a beard and smelled like air freshener, all I know," said Lupe Ramirez, the injured elf, a point guard on the eighth-grade basketball team.

That it had all come to this shouldn't have been a surprise. It was the rivalry's fault. Anyone with any sense in town knew Donnie and Eddie Lee's history—this was but a one-Bar-B-Q-joint town, after all—knew that there had been ill feeling between the two men, now hitting the lying side of their 40s, for a long time. They never made a public to-do about it, and, no, newcomers might not know this internecine history at all. Surely, though, Donnie and Eddie Lee had always been rivals, in a multitude of life's endeavors, best friends or no, which they had been, in high school.

As far back as Little League, they competed for the home run crown (and a chicken-fried steak dinner for two from Big Rig City), which Donnie captured one year, Eddie Lee the next. In high school, Donnie was named captain of the football team even though everybody said Eddie Lee hit a lot harder, made your teeth rattle. Donnie was voted Most Likely to Succeed and Most Handsome, and Eddie Lee,

Outstanding Young Farmer and vice president of the senior class. After graduating, Donnie plied his physical talents, and they were many at 6-2, 225, for the Longhorns on glorious Saturday afternoons in Austin. Everybody said he was a surefire pro prospect, until he blew out his knee his senior year.

Eddie Lee, meanwhile, decided to put off college for a while, and stayed home to farm his sick daddy's dry-land cotton and tend a motley collection of livestock, pets mostly. One weekend, with nothing better to do, he convinced Donnie's sweetheart, Louella, the senior band majorette and soon-to-be salutatorian, to run off to Mexico and get married. Donnie should've written more, she reasoned, and, besides, she loved kids.

Years tumbled by. Eddie Lee's daddy died and he and Louella had to put off college. In fact, they never escaped the farm, slaves to struggling crops and bank notes. Louella learned to plow a row as straight as any man, but she still clung to deeper desires. She wanted to open a little gift shop in town, to run something of her own, but the bank didn't. She found work at the parts department at the Chevrolet house each December, helping inventory, but that was about it for career advancement. Mostly, she cared for the house and the animals, for she and Eddie Lee never quite got around to having kids, either. She did get an occasional letter from Donnie, which she kept hidden in her dead mama's Bible in the bottom of the cedar chest, but she never saw him when he made his annual trip home at Christmas to visit his parents.

Donnie had missed a few turns in life, himself. His wife, sweetheart of his old fraternity, left him for nobody, which was somewhat worse than somebody. But for the insult, he wasn't all that upset, or surprised. He became reasonably happy being just another Austin lawyer, divorced and bored, with four bratty kids in overpriced private school, including one in rehab and another gravely into body piercing. Donnie, like so many Austin attorneys, made his serious money by lobbying besotted legislators in dark restaurants, a task about as difficult as teaching a chihuahua to grow ears.

Seeking a more honorable and challenging calling, he moved to the West Coast, where he used his football connections to secure a position with one of the nation's top sports management agencies, Maguire and Associates. There, he found instant success, but also learned that greed and buffoonery were not solely an affliction of Texas pols, and that instant-rich jocks were even more insufferably arrogant.

When his youngest daughter came home one day with three rings hanging from her left eyebrow—raising the family scoreboard to four for four—he said enough. He decided to move back to Funston City, to start life afresh.

He wasn't rock-star rich, but close enough. He built the biggest house in town, a three-story prairie Gothic, and, mostly for a hobby, bought a couple of nearby sections to farm. He also bought a blue-and-silver customized van, so he and the kids could do something wholesome together—like go see the Dallas Cowboys play, his passion since the Don Meredith days.

As a part-timer with good Mexican help, Donnie became an accomplished, respected farmer, and twice beat out Eddie Lee, a virtual green thumb even on mediocre land, for the honor of bringing in the county's first bale of cotton. For that, you got a hundred-dollar check and your and the bale's picture in the Star. But it meant far more than that, this first bale; it meant you knew how to work the land, how to sweet-talk it out of its riches, no matter the drought and insects and the cost of crop-dusting pesticides. It meant you knew what you were doing, were talented, were, at least in West Texas farm country, somebody the bankers would sit up for. Donnie was somebody already. This irked Eddie Lee to no end, particularly after he awoke one delicious spring day to find a note pinned to his pillow, Louella gone. "I'm sorry," it said, and that was it. She had finally found career advancement in Mr. Donnie Trappers, who lived just five miles down the road, in the biggest house in Funston City with four—four!—bathrooms and a three-car garage.

Except for a brief meeting at the Dairy Queen, a week after she left, Eddie Lee never tried to change her mind, never talked to her again, and never looked back. But he had never known such hurt, or disconnectedness. He took to serious alcohol and drank himself to public embarrassment, and spent night after sorry night in bare-bulb motels, in Lubbock, Abilene, Odessa, anywhere there might be a soft sanctuary he would never remember. After a year or so, the storm passed, he would remarry, adopt three children, and divorce, and then marry and divorce yet again.

One day, when he could think of no further way to abuse body or soul, he sobered up, which didn't mean he quit the bottle, necessarily. He simply made a list of everything that made him happy, and sad. He decided to make some changes, like no whiskey before 6 and no more late-child-support arguments. Baby steps. He even thought he might start going to church, once or twice a month, maybe. He had always had a healthy respect for religion and its potential consequences. It was just, like marriage, that he was never sure what exactly to look for, what to bring to the experience, and whether it was enhancing his well-being. But something was working. The clouds had broken for him, and he had experienced an awakening. Not that he had secured full inner calm, lasting peace, no, not truly, for he had long been infused with the gauzy recognition that there was always a big house just down the road, no matter where he was.

Soon, however, Eddie Lee learned that true happiness can be both negotiable and relative, and can arrive on the wings of a buzzard as well as a dove. This he realized when a man of profuse excitement in greasy khakis pounded on his door in the middle of the night and announced, "Aw-aw-aw-aw-awlllll! Aw-aw-aw-aw-awllllll! Yo-yo-yo-you s-s-st-st-struck awllllll!" It was a Cadillac of oil wells, on his back property line. Suddenly, he was introduced to a new slant of happy. First royalty check, he put a down payment on his dream house, three stories, with lots of gables and gingerbread and a porch all around, like his grandmother's was, and right next door to Louella and Donnie's. It had three more bathrooms than theirs. Townspeople whispered about what a divorced man did with seven bathrooms.

That was six years earlier, the first year he entered Funston City's Christmas display contest. Eddie Lee won third place, with an acrylic-painted plywood Nativity scene. He got $25 from the Chamber of Commerce and his picture in the Star. The judges said it was the delicately crafted features of the Baby Jesus, especially the blue eyes, that impressed them. He had talent, they said. He was somebody, and clearly a man of God. That was the year he pledged himself to designing bigger and better Christmas displays, year after year.

Mrs. Santa Claus, taking a break from Nativity peacekeeping duties, retreated to her third-floor master bedroom, from which she could survey all the evening's festivities below. The police had just left, and maybe things would quiet for a while, quiet as things ever get during the holidays. Some days, frankly, she wished for the quiet of Eddie Lee's farm, especially at Christmas, so she could just sling a few icicles on some scrawny tree and be done with it. At least there'd be no sullen stepkids, whose only redeeming social value was that they hated going to Cowboys games as much as she did. Trouble was, if she were back on the farm, that would mean she would still be married to Eddie, who was indeed a good man, someone she even cared about, still, in a kicked-puppy sort of way. Sometimes she thought, purely as an intellectual exercise, that their marriage went south the day she stuck the old John Deere tractor axle-deep in the bar ditch, and all she could do was sit there and cry, even though she was only a quarter-mile from the house. She had thought, too, that maybe the demise of the gift shop dream was what broke her spirit, begging at the bank. But, no, that wasn't it, neither. More than likely it was nothing more than what she told him in the Dairy Queen, right after she left him, years ago:

"I don't know what it is, Eddie Lee. It's not the farm. It's not even you. I just don't know exactly."

"It's about the kids, isn't it?" he said.

"No, no, no."

"I know it is. Look, we'll adopt. A whole houseful."

"No, Eddie Lee, I learned to live with that, long time ago."

"We'll go to that home in Fort Worth, tomorrow, make application."

"Eddie Lee, you don't understand. That's not it."

"Well, what, pray tell, might it be? You don't just run off in the middle of the night, not in a little town like this. People talk."

"Eddie Lee, maybe it was my daddy's fault. He always said, learn to type, you'll never have to worry."

"Your daddy was a smart man."

"Eddie Lee, I've forgotten how to type."

And with that she ran out of the Dairy Queen and Eddie Lee's life forever.

Later, Louella nearly died when Eddie Lee moved next door, just to spite her. She begged Donnie to sell and move, but Donnie said no way, period, just ignore him at all costs.

"If he ever tries anything funny," Donnie said, "I'll slap a lawsuit on him so fast it'll turn him cross-eyed."

Now, these many years later, as she preened before her vanity only hours after a neighbor goose was found dead in a manger, as she adjusted her white furry Mrs. Claus hat, Louella couldn't know that, just a ho-ho-ho away, in another third-floor bedroom, this one darkened, Eddie Lee was watching, confounded, trying to remember what he said wrong at the Dairy Queen, all those years ago.

Maybe it was the silvery full moon. Maybe it was youthful hormones, just waiting to misdirect. Maybe it was the Lord's will, but it's doubtful. Most likely, as Chief Dim Whittleton reconstructed matters, it was a flat tire and errant sugar cookies that caught most of the blame. Of course, the stink bomb under the manger didn't help.

Being Saturday night, the line of cars was unusually long and slow. That's when somebody had a flat, stopping traffic. Soon cars were honking and kids in cars suddenly realized they weren't there yet and weren't going to be anytime soon, thus becoming uncommonly irritable. Many parents just turned them loose, let them proceed to the yard displays. Some parents even abandoned their vehicles altogether. Some 30 teen-age boys on a bus from a local state juvenile facility, making a routine field trip in the continuing efforts to integrate them back into society, grew impatient and overpowered their driver, and drove the bus through neighboring yards to reach their destination.

And it came to pass that Donnie and Eddie Lee's yards were run amok with humanity. It was then that somebody threw a stink bomb from Donnie's yard into the Nativity scene, landing just behind the Virgin Mary, who had been sick at her stomach all week anyway. Eddie Lee, playing Joseph for the night as the regular Joseph was playing in a basketball tournament, told her to suck it up.

"I think I'm going to faint," the Virgin declared, and faint she did, startling the sheep, now gorged on sugar cookies, one of which had just thrown up on one of the angel's white beaded moccasins. As the sheep bolted, they disconcerted Saul the donkey, who, braying profoundly, booted one of the buffaloes in the chops and tore away from his stake. He then proceeded to kick and bray his way furiously across the lawn, rampaging through the story of Baby Jesus told in 30,000 lights. Two of the shepherds were crying, one was cursing to high heaven. Meanwhile, Saul, irreparable typographical errors strewn in his wake, reversed course, and headed down the driveway toward the yard next door. In his first act of defiance, Saul promptly kicked over the hot chocolate station, drenching three junior high elves.

Santa was livid. Little kids were screaming and mamas crying. The donkey was ruining his yard, his displays. Somebody with a pellet rifle was taking pot shots at the "Holiday Cheers!" lights, and grown women were helping themselves to the colored lights in his mesquites. Then a couple of boys from the bus, two of the more misunderstood ones, grew tired of waiting in line for the train and hijacked it, then derailed the little steamer at high speed, plowing through three 8-foot plywood elves. Santa wished he had his shotgun. All he could think of was Eddie Lee. He went to find him, quick.

Eddie Lee wasn't faring much better. The Virgin Mary was still prostrate, and the animals, except the goat, which was eating the swaddling clothes with Baby Jesus still attached, had scattered. One of the shepherds, named Emily, was saying it was all her fault, but nobody was listening. Worse, Eddie Lee's two towering red crosses were perilously swaying, like goal posts after an upset. And the `E' in `PEACE' had suddenly gone dark. At that moment, Joseph hated Santa. If only he could get his hands on him, now.

They met at the end of the brick wall that separated their yards, head to head, colliding in what passed for full speed. They jumped up, huffing, even madder.

"C'mon, Donnie, put 'em up. Let's settle this now."

Donnie was favoring his bum knee. "My pleasure."

They circled each other, their dukes up, for what seemed like minutes. Somebody yelled, "Hey, these two old geezers are getting it on," and a crowd began to gather. Santa and Joseph continued to circle, each imploring the other to swing first, each dredging up insults. The crowd egged them on.

"You're an embarrassment to your religion," Santa said.

"Leave my religion out of it. You'd a-never won that first bale without Mexican help."

"Hypocrite."

"Sinner," said Eddie Lee.

"Incompetent."

"Wife-stealer."

"Impotent incompetent."

"Say what?" said Eddie Lee.

By this time, the crowd was three deep around them, and beginning to snicker. "Better get with it — here comes the police," somebody hollered. With that, Santa and Joseph of Nazareth got it on, kind of. Though there were a fair number of swings and punches, nothing ever connected of any consequence. Mostly they just groped and tussled and wrestled and insulted each other. A pillow fight would have done more damage.

Finally, they backed away, eyeing each other not three feet apart, out of breath desperately, both arms cocked for their last half-hearted swings. It was then that Mrs. Santa arrived on the scene, running full speed, and jumped on Santa's back. Santa was actually in mid-throw when he felt the weight hit his back. His punch never landed, but he did, face down on the ground, Mrs. Santa on top. Joseph, who also missed with his haymaker, lost his balance and fell into the pile of Santas, hitting his nose on the back of Mrs. Santa's head. They were too exhausted to get up, all of them.

"Eddie Lee," Santa said, in a little voice of contrition from the bottom of the pile. "You think we embarrassed ourselves enough tonight?"

"No more than usual," Eddie Lee said, wiping his nose. "Let's do it again tomorrow, and charge admission."

And that's how the police found them, Mr. and Mrs. Santa and Joseph of Nazareth lying in a pile, giggling, carrying on a fairly cordial conversation, like they did this for sport routinely. A rivulet of blood dripped down Joseph's robe.

The next day was a busy one. Eddie Lee and Donnie repaired their displays and salvaged what they could. Eddie Lee's pride and joy, the two towering crosses with red bulbs, were not so towering anymore, and had to be drastically shortened. ON EARTH P ACE, its lights still running right to left, now stretched across the side yard between the two crosses, now not much taller than the lighted letters. Eddie Lee knew his chances of winning the yard display award were about as good as him slipping through the eye of a needle.

That afternoon they met with Chief Whittleton, at his request. They were expecting coffee and chitchat, but what the chief served was something far more substantial.

"Boys," he said, "I'll get to the point. I've knowed you two all your lives, was good friends with your folks. Now I'm going to give you some good old Dutch uncle advice: Eddie Lee, grow up. Donnie, get off your high horse. It's time to put the past away. Here's my deal: You either start speaking and acting like regular neighbors, or I'm gonna lock you both up. If you don't think I can do it, you'd better think again. The embarrassment you brought on our little town the other night—I could throw away the key, if I wanted.

"Boys, I have coffee at Big Rig two, three times a day, six days a week. I sure would like to see you two fellas, and the Missus, too, Donnie, drinking coffee together, laughing, visiting like normal people. Say, three times a week I wanna bump into you there.

"And another thing: I sure would like to see our little courthouse gussied up a bit. How do you think them red crosses would look hanging over the doors, Eddie Lee? I've already talked to the judge. He thinks they would look right nice, and maybe even put the fear of God into some of the prisoners across the street. Now, these two things would do my constitution a world of good. OK? That a deal, my friends?"

A deal, they said. In a way, they were both relieved.

When the Funston City Star hit the streets on Monday, there was a small story on Page One about Donnie and Eddie Lee's yard scenes:

FUNSTON CITY (Dec. 16) — Police Chief Dim Whittleton says he's solved the case of the dead goose in the manger which had many people worrying about possible local cult activity.

The chief said one of the shepherds confessed to being responsible for the goose's demise on Dec. 14 in Mr. Eddie Lee Madley's yard display. Chief said the shepherd, who the Star will not name because of his age, dropped the goose behind the donkey, also known as Saul, when he was putting up the animals for the night. The donkey spooked and kicked the goose, also known as Lucy, and sent the little feathered friend to her rich reward. The shepherd explained that he placed the goose in the manger because it looked like she was sleeping, and he thought that would be a fitting tribute to one who gave her all at Christmastime.

Meanwhile, the chief said, several lights were broken at Mr. Madley's and

*next door at Mr. Donald Trappers' yard
scenes, because of overflow crowds last
Saturday night. The chief also said an
abandoned 32-passenger bus was found
in Doc Ivory's swimming pool. But
otherwise the night was calm and a good
time was had by all.*

That night, Monday night, Santa and Mrs.
Claus invited Eddie Lee into their home. A
gentle breakthrough. Santa wanted to watch a
little Monday Night Football with Eddie Lee,
maybe reminisce. Eddie, though, only wanted
to talk about his shattered displays, the wholly
inadequate ON EARTH P ACE and the sad story
of Baby Jesus told in 30,000 lights, shattered
beyond salvation. On TV, the Cardinals and the
Rams were playing like Christmas, each trying
to gift the game to the other. A high shot from
the Goodyear blimp showed the stadium to be
only half full.

"Think I know how they feel," Eddie Lee
said. "You get so tired of losing. If I was the
coach of them teams, think I'd get up in that
blimp and take a jump."

"Eddie," Donnie said. "Maybe we could make
the final game next week. It's Cowboys and
Giants, for the championship. Monday night,
the last game. What you say? We'll leave the
kids in charge of the yards."

"Nah," Eddie said, blanching at the thought of Donnie's kids being in charge of anything short of piercing various body parts. "That's the night after judging night. I don't think I'll feel like going off, celebrating. Thank you kindly, though. If you and Louella want to go, I'll help watch your yard."

Later, near midnight, Donnie bolted upright in bed. He reached for the phone, and dialed Los Angeles.

"Jerry, Jerry Maguire. Donnie here. Donnie Trappers . . . calling from Texas. Say, it's been a long time . . . Say, I have a favor . . . You're tight with those Monday Night Football folks, right . . . ?"

On Page One of the *Funston City Star*, the following Monday afternoon, the headline read:

Local Man Madley Wins Display Award, Vows to Use Aggie Secret Weapon in Future

And the story:

FUNSTON CITY (Dec. 23) — Eddie Lee Madley, prominent local citizen, took first place in the Christmas Yard Display this year with a scene that literally glowed from the heavens.

Said head judge Molly McCann of Abilene, "The competition was a real close call, until those lights literally sprang out of the clouds—ON EARTH PEACE. We don't know how he did it, but ours was not to wonder why. They must of been a thousand feet up. And the symbolism was almost daunting."

Mr. Madley was mum as to how he did his trick, saying it was a trade secret, which he didn't fully understand himself. Meanwhile, the Star has learned that a well-known corporate blimp was seen in the area in the last 24 hours, making a brief stop at Abilene, on its way to Dallas for a football game. Company officials could not be reached for comment.

Mr. Madley won $500 in gift certificates, while Mr. Donald Trappers took second ($100 in certificates) and Jay Bradley III third (a $25 coupon to Big Rig City).

Mr. Madley said he is thrilled to win his first contest and vowed to make an even more spectacular display for next holiday season.

"I really can't talk about it now," he said, "but a couple of famous Aggie scientists have committed to developing my Chia Baby Jesus idea. They're real excited, and think they can make the Baby's eyes and swaddling clothes a reddish-purple, like those new bluebonnets."

Texas A&M horticulturists declined to comment, although a spokeswoman did say they were real intrigued.*

Above the story was a photograph of the winning yard, and in the far background, almost cut out of the photo, Mrs. Santa and Eddie Lee were arm in arm, next to Santa, who was pointing at the sky. You could almost hear the laughter. ✦U✦

Reprinted with permission of the Fort Worth Star-Telegram

The Cowboys' Christmas Ball
To the Ranchmen of Texas

By Larry Chittenden

The "poet-ranchman of Texas," William Lawrence "Larry" Chittenden (1862–1934), was born in Montclair, N.J., but came to Texas in his early 20s, working as a traveling dry-goods salesman and sending articles back to New York newspapers. In 1887, he and his uncle established the Chittenden Ranch in West Texas' Jones County, seven miles northwest of Anson, where he attended a Christmas dance for ranchers and cowboys at the Star Hotel. This was the inspiration for his best-known poem, "The Cowboys' Christmas Ball," which first appeared in 1890 in Anson's Texas Western *newspaper and was later included in Chittenden's first volume of* Ranch Verses *in 1893. An annual reenactment of the dance has been held in Anson since 1934. Singer Michael Martin Murphey recorded "The Cowboys' Christmas Ball" in 1985.*

Way out in Western Texas, where the Clear
    Fork's waters flow,
Where the cattle are "abrowzin'," an' the
    Spanish ponies grow;
Where the Northers "come awhistlin'" from
    beyond the Neutral Strip;
And the prairie dogs are sneezin', as if they had
    "The Grip";
Where the cayotes come ahowlin' 'round the
    ranches after dark,

And the mockingbirds are singin' to the lovely
    "medder lark";
Where the 'possum and the badger, and
    rattlesnakes abound,
And the monstrous stars are winkin' o'er a
    wilderness profound;
Where lonesome, tawny prairies melt into airy
    streams,
While the Double Mountains slumber, in
    heavenly kinds of dreams;
Where the antelope is grazin' and the lonely
    plovers call—
It was there that I attended "The Cowboys'
    Christmas Ball."

The town was Anson City, old Jones's county
    seat,
Where they raised Polled Angus cattle, and
    waving whiskered wheat;
Where the air is soft and "bammy," an' dry an'
    full of health,
And the prairies is explodin' with agricultural
    wealth;
Where they print the Texas Western, that Hec.
    McCann supplies
With news and yarns and stories, of most
    amazin' size;
Where Frank Smith "pulls the badger," on
    knowin' tenderfeet,

And Democracy's triumphant, and mighty hard
    to beat;
Where lives that good old hunter, John Milsap,
    from Lamar,
Who "used to be the Sheriff, back East, in Paris
    sah!"
'T was there, I say, at Anson with the lovely
    "widder Wall,"
That I went to that reception, "The Cowboys'
    Christmas Ball."

The boys had left the ranches and come to town
    in piles;
The ladies—"kinder scatterin'"—had gathered
    in for miles.
And yet the place was crowded, as I remember
    well,
'T was got for the occasion, at "The Morning
    Star Hotel."
The music was a fiddle an' a lively tambourine,
And a "viol came imported," by the stage from
    Abilene.
The room was togged out gorgeous—with
    mistletoe and shawls,
And candles flickered frescoes, around the airy
    walls.
The "wimmin folks" looked lovely—the boys
    looked kinder treed,
Till their leader commenced yellin': "Whoa!
    fellers, let's stampede,"

And the music started sighin', an' awailin'
    through the hall
As a kind of introduction to "The Cowboys'
    Christmas Ball."

The leader was a feller that came from
    Swenson's ranch,
They called him "Windy Billy," from "little
    Deadman's Branch."
His rig was "kinder keerless," big spurs and
    highheeled boots;
He had the reputation that comes when "fellers
    shoots."
His voice was like a bugle upon the mountain's
    height;
His feet were animated an' a mighty, movin'
    sight,
When he commenced to holler, "Neow, fellers
    stake your pen!
"Lock horns ter all them heifers, an' russle 'em
    like men.
"Saloot yer lovely critters; neow swing an' let
    'em go,
"Climb the grape vine 'round 'em—all hands
    docedo!
"You Mavericks, jine the roundup—Jest skip
    her waterfall,"
Huh! hit wuz gettin' happy, "The Cowboys'
    Christmas Ball!"

The boys were tolerable skittish, the ladies
    powerful neat,
That old bass viol's music just got there with
    both feet!
That wailin', frisky fiddle, I never shall forget;
And Windy kept asingin'—I think I hear him
    yet—
"Oh X's, chase your squirrels, an' cut 'em to one
    side;
"Spur Treadwell to the centre, with Cross P
    Charley's bride;
"Doc Hollis down the middle, an' twine the
    ladies' chain;
"Varn Andrews pen the fillies in big T Diamond's
    train.
"All pull yer freight together, neow swallow
    fork an' change;
"'Big Boston,' lead the trail herd, through little
    Pitchfork's range.
"Purr 'round yer gentle pussies, neow rope 'em!
    Balance all!"
Huh! hit wuz gettin' active—"The Cowboys'
    Christmas Ball!"

The dust riz fast an' furious; we all jes' galloped
    'round,
Till the scenery got so giddy that T Bar Dick
    was downed.
We buckled to our partners, an' told 'em to hold
    on,

Then shook our hoofs like lightning, until the
    early dawn.
Don't tell me 'bout cotillions, or Germans. No
    sire 'ee!
That whirl at Anson City just takes the cake
    with me.
I'm sick of lazy shufflin's, of them I've had my
    fill,
Give me a frontier breakdown, backed up by
    Windy Bill.
McAllister ain't nowhar: when Windy leads the
    show,
I've seen 'em both in harness, and so I sorter
    know—
Oh, Bill, I sha'n't forget yer, and I'll oftentimes
    recall,
That lively gaited sworray—"The Cowboys'
    Christmas Ball."

A Christmas Story

By John Henry Faulk

*The gifted Texas storyteller, broadcaster, author, playwright and
activist John Henry Faulk recorded his Christmas story in 1974 for the
National Public Radio arts program "Voices in the Wind." Its reading
became a holiday tradition for NPR. Faulk died in 1990, but his legend
lives on, and it is hard to imagine a story that more purely embodies
the spirit of Christmas, wrapped in the hardscrabble country rhythms
of Texas speech.*

The day after Christmas a number of years ago,
I was driving down a country road in Texas.
And it was a bitter cold, cold morning. And
walking ahead of me on the gravel road was a
little bare-footed boy with non-descript ragged
overalls and a makeshift sleeved sweater tied
around his little ears. I stopped and picked him
up. Looked like he was about 12 years old and
his little feet were blue with the cold. He was
carrying an orange.

And he got in and had the brightest blue
eyes one ever saw. And he turned a bright smile
on my face and says, "I'm-a going down the road
about two miles to my cousins. I want to show
him my orange old Santa Claus brought me."
But I wasn't going to mention Christmas to him

because I figured he came from a family—the kind that don't have Christmas. But he brought it up himself. He said, "Did old Santa Claus come to see you, Mister?" And I said, "Yes. We had a real nice Christmas at our house and I hope you had the same."

He paused for a moment, looked at me. And then with all the sincerity in the world said, "Mister, we had the wonderfulest Christmas in the United States down to our place. Lordy, it was the first one we ever had had there. See, we never do have them out there much. Don't notice when Christmastime comes. We heared about it, but never did have one 'cause—well, you know, it's just papa says that old Santa Claus — papa hoorahs a lot and said old Santa Claus was scared to bring his reindeer down into our section of the county because folks down there so hard up that they liable to catch one of his reindeer and butcher him for meat. But just several days before Christmas, a lady come out from town and she told all the families through there, our family, too, that they was—old Santa Claus was come in town to leave some things for us and if papa'd go in town, he could get some Christmastime for all of us. And papa hooked up the mule and wagon. He went in town. But he told us children, said, "Now don't ya'll get all worked up and excited because there might not be nothing to this yarn that lady told."

And—but, shucks, she hadn't got out of sight up the lane there till we was done a-watching for him to come back. We couldn't get our minds on nothing else, you know. And mama, she'd come to the door once in a while and say, "Now y'all quit that looking up the lane because papa told you there might not be nothing." And—but long about the middle of the afternoon, well, we heared the team a-jangling harness a-coming and we ran out in the front yard, and Ernie, my little brother, called out and said, "Yonder come papa." And here come them mules just in a big trot, you know, and papa standing upright in the bed of that wagon holding two big old chickens, all the feathers picked off. And he was just yelling, "Merry Christmas. Merry Christmas." And the team stopped right in front of the gate. And all us children just went a-swarming out there like a flock of chichis, you know, and just a-crawling over that wagon and a-looking in.

And, Mister, I wish you could have seen what was in that wagon. It's bags of stripety candy and apples and oranges and sacks of flour and some real coffee, you know, and just all tinselly and pretty and we couldn't say nothing. Just kind of held our breath and looked at it, you know. And papa standing there just waving them two chickens, a-yelling, "Merry Christmas to you. Merry Christmas to you," and a-laughing that big old grin on his face. And mama, she come a-hurrying out with the baby in her arms, you know. And when she looked in that wagon, she just stopped, and then papa, he dropped them two chickens and reached and caught the baby out of her arms, you know, and held him up and said, "Merry Christmas to you, Santa Claus." And baby, little old Alvie Lee, he just laughed like he knowed it was Christmas, too, you know. And mama, she started telling us the name of all of them nuts. They wasn't just peanuts. They was—she had names for all of them. She— mama knows a heap of things like that. She'd seen that stuff before, you know? And we was, all of us, just a-chattering and a-going on at the same time, us young'uns, a-looking in there.

And all of a sudden, we heared papa call out, "Merry Christmas to you, Sam Jackson." And we stopped and looked. And here comes Sam Jackson a-leading that old cripple-legged mule of his up the lane. And papa said, "Sam Jackson, did you get in town to get some Christmas this year?" Sam Jackson, you know, he sharecrops over there across the creek from our place. And he shook his head and said, "Well, no, sir, Mister. Well, I didn't go in town. I heared about that, but I didn't know it was for colored folks, too. I thought it was just for you white families." All of a sudden, none of us children were saying nothing. Papa, he looked down at mama and mama looked up at him and they didn't say nothing, like they don't a heap of times, but they know what the other one's a-thinking. They're like that, you know. And all of a sudden, papa, he broke out in a big grin again. He said, "Dad-blame-it, Sam Jackson, it's a sure a good thing you come by here. Lord have mercy, I liked to forgot. Old Santa Claus would have me in court if he heared about this. The last thing he asked me if I lived out here near you. Said he hadn't seen you around and said he wanted me to bring part of this out here to you and your family, your woman and your children."

Well, sir, Sam Jackson, he broke out in a big grin. Papa says, "I'll tell you what to do. You get your wife and children and you come down here tomorrow morning. It's going to be Christmastime all day long. Come early and stay late." Sam Jackson said, "You reckon?" And mama called out to him and said, "Yes, and you tell your wife to be sure and bring some pots and pans because we're going to have a heap of cookin' to do and I ain't sure I've got enough to take care of all of it." Well, sir, old Sam Jackson, he started off a-leading that mule up the lane in a full trot, you know, and he was a-heading home to get the word to his folks and his children, you know.

And next morning, it just—you remember how it was yesterday morning, just rosy red and looked like Christmastime. It was cold, but you didn't notice the cold, you know, when the sun just come up, just all rosy red. And us young'uns were all out of bed before daylight seemed like, just running in the kitchen and smelling and looking. And it was all there sure enough. And here come Sam Jackson and his team and his wife and his five young'uns in there. And they's all lookin' over the edge. And we run out and yelled, "Merry Christmas. Merry Christmas." And papa said, "Christmas gift to you, Sam Jackson. Ya'll come on in." And they come in and mama and Sister Jackson, they got in the kitchen and they started a-cooking things up. And us young'uns started playing Christmastime. And it's a lot of fun, you know. We'd just play Christmas Gift with one another and run around and around the house and just roll in the dirt, you know, and then we started playing Go Up To The Kitchen Door And Smell. And we'd run up and smell inside that kitchen door where mama and Sister Jackson was a-cooking at, and then we'd just die laughing and roll in the dirt, you know, and go chasing around and playing Christmas Gift.

And we played Christmastime till we just wore ourselves out. And papa and Sam Jackson—they put a table up and put some sheets over it, some boards up over some sawhorses. And everybody had a place, even the baby. And mama and Sister Jackson said, "Well, now it's ready to come on in. We're going to have Christmas dinner." And I sit right next to Willy Jackson, you know, and he just rolled his eyes at me and I'd roll mine at him. And we'd just die laughing, you know, and there was an apple and an orange and some stripety candy at everybody's place. And that was just dessert, see. That wasn't the real Christmas dinner. Mama and them had done cooked that up. And they just had it spread up and down the table.

And so papa and Sam Jackson, they'd been sitting on the front porch and they come in. Papa, he sit at one end of the table, Sam Jackson sit at the other. And it was just a beautiful table like you never had seen. And I didn't know nothing could ever look like that and smell that good, you know. And Sam Jackson, you know, he's real black and he had on that white clean shirt of his and then them overalls. Everything had been washed and was real clean. Papa, he said, "Brother Jackson, I believe you're a deacon in the church. I ain't much of a church man myself, but I believe you're a deacon. Maybe you'd be willing to give grace." Well, Sam Jackson, he stood up there and his hands is real big and he kind of held onto the side of the table, you know. But he didn't bow his head like a heap of folks do when they're saying the blessing. He just looked up and smiled. And he said, "Lord, I hope you having as nice a Christmas up there with your angels as we're having down here because it sure is Christmastime down here.

And I just wanted to say Merry Christmas to you, Lord.

Like I say, Mister, I believe that was the wonderfulest Christmas in the United States of America." ✤

*Reprinted with permission of the
John Henry Faulk Estate*